GRITS IN THE GRAVEYARD

J. L. COLLINS

First Edition.

Cover design by Mariah Sinclair
at Maria Sinclair Book Cover Design

Witch Hazel Lane Mysteries Series Order:
Grits In The Graveyard (Book 1)
Devil On My Doorstep (Book 2)
Monsters Under The Magnolia (Book 3)

Keep track of J. L.'s new and upcoming book releases and join her fun giveaways, behind the scenes work, and occasional pictures of her dog!
Click Here!

For my DD sprint buddies-
SO. WORTH. IT.
<3

MORE FROM J. L. COLLINS

Keep track of J. L.'s new and upcoming book releases and join her fun giveaways, behind the scenes work, and occasional pictures of her dog!

Subscribe Here!

Spell Maven Mystery Series Order:

Spell Maven from Spell Haven (Book 1)

Snitch Witch (Book 2)

Tragic Magick (Book 3)

Witch Hazel Lane Mystery Series Order:

Grits in the Graveyard (Book 1)

Devil on My Doorstep (Book 2)

Monsters Under the Magnolia (Book 3)

1

WHAT HAPPENS IN VEGAS...

Illusions are to amuse the mundane mind, while real magic is used to ensnare an enlightened mind in possibilities. Or at least that's the way Grandmother would explain it to me. In other less haughtier words; magicians are just playing make-believe in a world full of the real stuff.

And the old hag had a point.

Magic acts were one of the top selling shows in Vegas, aside from Britney and Celine, of course. And I happened to have scored the best seat in the house at this show—my own.

I stepped my high-heeled foot onstage, ready for the first show of the evening.

Little did I know my timing couldn't have been any worse...

Honestly the night started like any other. My dressing room was practically sparkling clean thanks to my absolutely angelic assistant, Corinne. She knew about my need for organization and neatness in order to keep calm, and she saw to it that I got what I needed.

The costumes were all hanging, freshly dry-cleaned on the clothes rack with the various boots and heels all glittering from underneath. My notes and various pages of stage diagram and the like that inevitably ended up strewn all over the darn place were tucked neatly into folders she' made for me. Bottles of my favorite brand of water were lined up against the lighted vanity.

And not a single smudge on the mirror, mind you.

Yes, she was my saving grace. But when I walked into my dressing room, her usual calm and collected demeanor was gone. Corinne was the flurry in my room this time, pacing back and forth, her eyes wide.

I'd shut the door behind myself, frowning. "Corinne, darlin', are you all right? You're looking a little flushed there."

She shook her head, though it didn't seem such a conscious effort on her part. "Birdie. Birdie, we have a problem."

I stopped dead in my tracks. "We do? Well, now. I don't much like the sound of that." The honeyed drawl in my voice was strong whenever anxiety creeped into it. Old habits die hard, as they say.

Corinne held up her phone, where a video of a familiar-looking news anchor with his hands nervously splayed out on the desk in front of him, was going live. The headline emblazoned across the bottom of the screen had me blinking my false lashes so hard I was sure to need them re-applied.

WITCHES AMONG US - STARTLING PROOF DURING PRESS CONFERENCE.

Even though I was in my usual sneakers, I somehow managed to stumble as I took a step toward her. "What's this?" I whispered.

"I-I don't know, Birdie. There were some people who were giving a press conference somewhere in England, I think. They claimed to be part of some kind of organization..."

In my head, I silently pleaded with her not to say it.

"...like an organization of witches. They had a name, but I forgot it. It sort of sounded medieval. Like the Knights of the Round Table. The Order? No, the High-Order of Magic? Oh, it was something like that anyway. They looked like normal people, but then they did something. Everyone at the press conference was shouting, some people crying even. The camera cut out for a moment and then it was so strange. One of the men was levitating off the ground. There was nothing holding or pulling him up. Birdie, you have to believe me."

The blood went cold in my veins. So the High-Order had the brass ones to go public. Had I missed the memo? None of my connections had said anything about this happening... Yet here we were. The rest of the world now paused, collectively wondering what to do now.

And I didn't want to know the answer one way or the other. It was my own experience that whenever you stood out for something you couldn't help, others were there on your tail, ready to bring you down into the shadows.

I fixed my gaze on Corinne who was clearly shaken up by this announcement. "Leave those folks to whatever they claim to be, and let's focus on what we can control. And that's our first show tonight, right darlin'?"

She nodded. "But what about you? Aren't you worried?"

We both knew what she meant. She'd never come right out and said it, but I knew she was a smart girl. She'd figured out the truth not long after I started working my shows there at the MGM Grand.

"I'll figure it out. No need to fret over me. I can handle myself." I flashed her my best smile and she seemed to relax a little. "Now, would you help me pick which earrings to wear tonight? I'm thinking the diamonds . . . what do you think?"

The thunderous applause had welcomed me as I'd pushed past the curtains and stepped into the spotlight. The thrumming, deep bass echoed throughout the MGM Grand's million-dollar sound system, followed by the same ethereal tune that announced my arrival to all the good folks who came to see me and my tricks. And I stood there under the heat of the stage lights, ready to dazzle them all.

Well, that was my *intention* anyway.

I was all ready for my set. The lights were on their cues perfectly, and I waved at everyone in the crowd. "Well hello to all of you fine people, tonight!" I shouted into the lav mic pinned on my collar. "I do hope you prepared yourself for a night of exquisite fun!" I smiled at the cheers. Not that my ego needed more stroking of course, but all the same...

Despite the worry starting to gnaw on the other thoughts in my brain, I put on one of my best performances yet. The illusionist in me soaked up the gasps from the audience like a sponge ready to be wrung out. They ooh'ed and ahh'ed throughout much of the show, and I'd wiped at my forehead for a moment to ease into the next trick, the words on the edge of my tongue.

Then the boos came.

I'd had a few of them here and there over the nearly four years I'd been here in Vegas. Even though half the strip's occupants were drunk after five PM, they were mostly polite to me.

But these were different. Louder, and echoing throughout the theater. It was like the whole atmosphere of my show had changed. There was a low chanting I couldn't quite pick up spreading across the seats. Others were looking around, bewildered, turning in their seats and whispering to each other.

I blinked and wiped at my forehead again, shielding my eyes from the bright spotlight to see just what the heck was going on. "Get on out of here! These other kind people paid good money to be here too, you know!"

Witch. Witch. Witch.

My heart that had been racing was ready to jump out of my throat. Memories flooded past the gnawing worry. I screeched at them all, begging them to stop, and before I knew what I was doing, I had pushed past the side curtains doing my very best not to get sick all over myself. They were Louboutin boots, after all.

I may not have been a rocket scientist, but I was particularly gifted in the knowledge of witch hunts. Especially being a witch myself.

With barely more than a suitcase packed, I had the keycards to my luxurious penthouse suite that had been my home for the past two years and practically flung them at the concierge as I went careening around the corner of the lobby.

"Miss Birdie! Where are you going?" he'd shouted after me from the front desk.

When you've been around as long as I have— for one-hundred and thirty-three years, thank you kindly— you learn the way a proper southern lady would handle such a nasty surprise as this. You learn to keep your wits about you, or you learn to play possum.

I, on the other hand, had no choice but to go with the third option.

Running for the hills.

VEGAS ILLUSIONIST BIRDIE LOSES HER MIND AND HER GIG AT THE MGM GRAND

Where before you couldn't look in the general direction of the infamous hotel without seeing her name in lights somewhere, the woman who goes by simply 'Birdie' has seemed to both fallen from grace and gone into hiding.

'Birdie - Magnolia Magic,' as the show was aptly named, was a magic show fit for a king, only performed by a true southern belle. Her last season's shows all sold out four months in advance. There were even rumors swirling around of Birdie getting her own Netflix Original series, beating out potential competition from the likes of Criss Angel and Michael Carbonaro for the spot.

After the events of her last show on Saturday evening, everything has changed.

Over two-thousand people with tickets for Birdie's showings on Saturday, September 29th, were issued refunds at the box office after the show was cancelled.

Five people had to be escorted out by security during the first show for disrupting the act. These audience members began to disrupt her by loudly repeating a single word —'witch.' One of these five people was ultimately arrested for public intoxication and resisting arrest. The self-proclaimed illusionist screamed and appeared unhinged, according to many witnesses, before she stormed off mid-show after the chanting. From there, the stagehands working that night claim Birdie tore through the off-stage and screamed at others as she headed out of the theater and up to her penthouse.

Her manager, Preston McDonald, has issued an apology on her behalf, asking that her fans give her time to decompress after a 'particularly grueling' tour. When asked if the rumors of Birdie leaving town were true, Mr. McDonald fumbled for an answer before declining to comment after all.

We have to wonder. Has Birdie lost her momentum after just hitting her stride? And where has she run off to?

October 1st, 2019 - TheDailyGossip.com

2

GONE ROGUE

"Oh, you know. Around." I fished the lip stick from my purse, applying it with a steady hand in the car visor's mirror. You can't go wrong with a color named *Belle of the Ball.*

Preston sighed. "You can't just go off the grid like this. Not without telling me, anyway. How am I supposed to get ahold of you? Carrier pigeon?"

I rolled my eyes and slapped the visor shut. "I am allowed to go off on my own accord, you know. We may have a contract, but you can't *chain me to a tree somewhere until this whole thing dies down,* as you put it."

Through the dusty windshield, I could just make out the sign up ahead.

Welcome to Mississippi - Birthplace of America's Music!

I grit my teeth, forcing myself to relax as I pushed against the gas pedal. Once upon a time, I told myself I'd never see this sign again.

"Birdie, are you even listening to me? I have the Board of Directors at the MGM in my ear, demanding to know where their star has run off to. They're livid as hell - I've got thousands of ticket sales being yanked out of our very pockets! What am I supposed to tell everyone? You've gone rogue? You can't back out like this. As you mentioned, you do have a contractual obligation to fill and Birdie I will say that as your manager, I think it's best that—"

His voice went silent as I tapped the little red button on my phone and tossed the darn thing into the passenger seat. Preston hadn't always been such a sniveling excuse for a man. Kowtowing with all of Las Vegas' finest was something he'd only just caught up to ever since we booked our tour at the MGM Grand. When I was just another magician trying to pay her bills, he was just as sweet as cherry pie. It was sad, really.

Not that I had any room to talk. Me harping on poor Preston wasn't much different than a pot calling the kettle black. It wasn't just the fame that got to my head—it was Vegas and all her glory. I was able to keep a certain mystique about myself, considering no one ever saw me outside the shows. Celebrities, politicians, journalists, they all wanted to meet me in person from time to time—to find out who was behind the young and beautiful mask with the magic tricks.

If only they knew. There was nothing young about me at this point. Maybe my spirit. Though even that was taking a good tarnishing from time to time.

I only just noticed that the fine lines in my hands were starting to really bug me. I glanced down at them on the steering wheel. I used to tell myself that I would find ways to cover up my age, that I'd do whatever it took. I'd seen Grandmother and the severity of time in her face and skin. It used to be that I wanted to avoid it all. To blend in with the younger, beautiful people.

But Vegas had shown me that it was *all* just a mask. So I made my own mask—a potion recipe I'd found in an underground witch market—and wore it every night as I performed my shows. It was still me, still my face even… just a younger me. The version of myself that was around in oh, let's say 1910. I was only twenty-four back when I was out on my own without my family thankfully, and I was known by my full given name. Nella, Mississippi was the furthest thing from Miss Birdie Hyacinth Devaine's mind back then.

I checked the clock on the dash. If I hurried, I'd be in Nella just in time for lunch.

With the Beatles' White album on full melodious blast, I pulled up to my next destination after popping into a diner on the outskirts of town. Finishing off the last bits of my fried green tomatoes in the greasy paper bag, I smiled. If I knew Preston, my bank account would be frozen if he didn't hear from me in the next twenty-four hours. Which meant I only had one day to get this done.

"Lady Luck be on my side old girl," I muttered as I slid out of the car.

My first impression of the office was that it was made to be modern with clean lines and subtle accent colors. Boring, really.

"Hello, ma'am. Did you have an appointment?" the short woman behind the tidy front desk asked, putting on a polite smile that just barely reached her eyes.

"Oh, not quite. Is that… will that be okay?"

"Absolutely. Are you selling or buying?"

"Buying, it looks like. And hoping to do it quickly to boot."

She nodded. "Of course. If you'll take a seat, I'll have one of our realtors come out to meet you. And what was your name?"

For a moment I imagined myself giving her some nom de

plume, but I rattled ahead without giving it another thought. "Birdie Devaine."

"Someone will be right with you Miss Devaine," she said before turning on her heel.

Truth be told, I had no idea what the heck I was doing here. My mind was racing as I called upon a reasonable answer. Nope. There was none. My eyes flickered toward the door. *This is a dumber than dirt idea. Maybe I still have time to figure out something else—*

"Miss Devaine?"

I snapped to, blinking up at the young man standing there with his hand all ready to shake mine. "Yes?" I said, giving him a firm shake. I've been around enough to know how men tend to treat women on their own in need of some kind of service not completely understood.

He gave me a smile that could have sold teeth whitener by the truckload. "Wonderful to meet you. My name's Gregory Barnaby. Grace says you're looking to purchase a property?"

I stood up tall. Chalk another tally for Christian Louboutin—these boots were made for this very occasion. "I am."

He gestured for me to follow him into the office where he went over the usual rigamarole. As rude as it may have been to Mr. Barnaby, I was only half-listening. Something was pushing me to hurry up this whole process, and I knew better than to go against my gut.

"If you're free Miss Devaine, I can show you some more properties as alternatives. You're sure you want to only look here in Nella? Not in any of the surrounding areas? If you're willing, we could maybe expand outside the county to—"

"No, no. That'll be all right. I know exactly which property I'm interested in, as I've shown you here," I said, pointing to the print-out he'd done for me. "I don't even need to take a look first. I'm willing to buy it up now without all the hassle, if you please."

He made a funny face but shrugged and leaned forward over the small stack of papers on his desk. "The Hampton House it is, then. It's in need of renovations, and the coding inspector for the town will need to come out and take a look at it before you sign the dotted line. But as it's been unclaimed by the former residents, the town has it up for auction within the next few months. Unless you are absolutely sure this is the house you want? Sight unseen?"

"I am absolutely sure. This is the price, correct?" I glanced down at the printout.

He nodded. "Yes ma'am."

The smaller plantation home in the photo didn't look much different than it had in 1901. With the exception of the paved drive and dilapidated shutters hanging off their hinges, of course.

"Let's call the good inspector. I've got a mighty large check to write it seems," I added smoothly, itching to get this show on the road.

"Certainly." Mr. Barnaby tucked something into his blazer's pocket and smiled. "After you."

With my fingers crossed I waited for the bank's say-so at the table. It's funny how things can move so fast and so slow at the same time. Back in Vegas, life was like riding a rocket that exploded into the brightest fireworks you've ever seen, only to come crashing back down from each flight. Here in Nella however, life moved slower than molasses.

Except for, apparently, buying a beat-up old house on its last leg. I found this out a few hours later.

"Well, Miss Devaine. It looks like you got yourself a deal!" Mr. Barnaby tapped his finger to the blue file containing all of the Hampton House's important information. With flourish, he presented the house keys to me.

Anxious excitement zipped up my spine as I took them, and the reality of the situation was still not registering.

I just bought a house. And not just any house—but *the*

house. The house I'd always dreamed of, growing up on the poor side of Nella just past the train tracks behind the church.

It would need work. The kind of work I couldn't use magic for—the nitty gritty, dirt under your fingernails type of work. I couldn't remember the last time I'd done anything like that. Not with the conveniences of modernity, any who.

Slipping back into my car, I stared at the time, lost in thought. "All I need now is to scoot the rest of my funds to a different account… make sure that sucker doesn't drain me dry so I can afford the materials and maybe even some food for myself…"

A plan was forming in my head. One that didn't involve magic for the first time in a rather *long* time.

3
SIGHT UNSEEN

I lied. This was most definitely going to involve magic. Oodles of it, quite possibly.

"Oh my word, Birdie, what have you gotten yourself into?" I whispered to myself, standing at the edge of Hampton House's shadow. It stretched toward me bit by bit until the toes of my shoes were swallowed up by it.

The house had been standing at 32 Witch Hazel Lane since before I was born—built by Rudolf Hampton in the 1870s if memory served me. The Hampton family was one of the wealthier families when I was growing up, Rudolf made his money from the sole textile mill in Mississippi at the time. And with the coming of industry to the south, ever so slowly, the Hamptons had really racked up the dough by the time I'd left at fifteen.

It was one of those beautiful houses that spoke of the future at the time. By today's standards of course, it was an architectural relic. A Queen Anne build, with a mix of steeped and gabled roofs and its three-story bay window that was topped off by a turret—it was definitely out of place with the newer build around it.

I glanced around the neighborhood to see how it had changed, but my eyes were immediately drawn back to the house.

Yes, it was an old forlorn-looking thing to be sure. But its gables, the gothic revival styled shutters, the spire on the towered bay window and the wrap-around veranda with the beautiful lattice were straight out of my childhood dreams. I lost count of how many times I'd find myself taking a short detour on the way back home from running errands for Grandmother—just to stop and stare at the massive home looming over the rest of street. The fact was there wasn't a house in Nella that held a candle to the Hampton House.

Of course… that was a very long time ago. Now the house didn't look so much like a blessing as it did a cursed thing, haunting the shadows of the overgrown patch of land it occupied.

I frowned as I took in the weeds choking out old flowerbeds around the gazebo. Landscaping wasn't really my forte. Sure, I'd done plenty of weeding and having to learn botany and herbalism was just part of everyday life, growing up as a witch. But when was the last time I actually had to get my hands dirty? It shamed me to think that I couldn't really remember.

"Whew boy, this is going to be one bumpy ride."

With Gregory due tomorrow evening to help me finish up the last of the deed paperwork, I had all day today and most of tomorrow to take a good look at my new abode. I slammed my old Mercedes' trunk shut, threw my duffle bag over my shoulder along with my purse, and yanked the suitcase over the curb.

I took stock of everything that caught my eye that needed fixing. Of course the grass was in need of mowing, the moss-covered fountain looked like it hadn't been churning out water in decades, and the gazebo's roof had a stray tree limb jutting out of it. Me and my suitcase both nearly flipped over as it snagged on a tree root breaking through the sidewalk.

I mumbled to myself and kept trucking up the stairs where I took extra caution with my steps over the warped wood. At one point, Hampton House's roof and steps had been a lovely shade of green, but now they looked dull and washed out.

Fishing out the key from my purse, I couldn't help but wonder if this wasn't my biggest most recent mistake.

"No, child. Marrying Ronnie was a mistake. This is a new adventure," I said aloud, knowing full well no one was around to hear me. One of my *quirkier* quirks.

The screen door was caked in rust and dirt and nearly hit my rear with the tight coil of it as I pulled it open. Shoving the key in, I twisted it and gave a gentle push. The main door creaked open with a groan like it was yawning awake, giving way to the foyer.

I sucked in a quick breath. Talk about a time warp. The old floors had been polished new even under the layer of dust. The wood trimming had all been refinished at one point. Careful not to drag my suitcase across the floor, I picked it up by the handle and placed everything on the empty bay window missing its cushion.

Dusting my hands off, I pushed my sunglasses back up over my head and took a real good look around. Lordy this place was in need of some serious TLC. And it wasn't the kind I could so easily afford anymore. I'd have to be frugal as all get out if I wanted to make this place into what I always imagined it to be. With the added modern conveniences like central A/C, for starters—there was no way I was willing to spend a single summer day in Mississippi without *that*.

Luckily for me, as I walked through the foyer and into the formal dining room, I noticed the thermostat gathering dust on the wall.

I'd already been down to the utility office downtown to set up my water and electricity for the place, and when I tapped on the little white box I was happy to see it light up.

"Yes, I think that'll do just fine."

The rest of the house was in pretty good condition, minus the general dinginess and griminess of the place. I shuddered to think what caused the fist-sized hole leading in and out of the large pantry in the kitchen.

I ran my hand along the staircase's railing as I went up. "I'm going to have to check out the previous occupants sometime. For a place that's in such disrepair outside, the inside isn't so bad."

Upstairs was much the same. Five bedrooms, two of them smaller and set off to the back of the house. Probably for servants, if memory served. There were a few ragged sheers hanging in the windows here and there, and the rest of the place was bare bones empty. I could live with that.

It was definitely going to take some doing, but as I hoisted the windows in the master bedroom open, I felt like maybe I could do it after all.

My phone buzzed in my hand while I was working on my to do list, jingling with an old Charleston rag-time cover. Preston's name covered my screen and I rolled my eyes as I dismissed the call and got right back to it. I'd have to put that man out of my head for a little while if I was going to get some work done around here. If I was going to answer the phone for anyone, it would be my sweet Corinne.

I tapped my finger against my chin, looking around kitchen. "They may have kept up the maintenance on this place but surely they could've done with a newer oven? I swear I saw this very same model in an old Sears catalog in 1974."

I leaned against the Formica countertop, drumming my unkempt nails along it. In my head I pictured a farmhouse style kitchen, complete with an old copper deep basin sink. The small sink we had in our old run-down place over the tracks had a chipped porcelain sink to go with the chipped porcelain tub and the chipped tiles under our feet.

I would make this place better than all that.

Fresh linens in the sitting room, maybe turn that hole in the roof above the staircase into a skylight…

Something pulled me out of my thoughts, and I looked down the hallway to where I'd just shut the door to the servants back stairway. There was a heavy scratching coming from the other side of the door, pushing it hard against the lock.

I jumped back, my eyes wide. What in the name of Dixie was that? Quickly looking for the nearest wieldable weapon, I grabbed one of the only things left in the house from the wall—a former gaslit sconce—and held the heavy brass thing over my head as I crept back down the hall.

The scratching continued, this time followed by a piteous whine. I frowned. That didn't sound like a person at all. In fact, it sounded like…

The door burst open all at once, sending splintered wood and the remnants of the door's lock scattered across the kitchen, and sending me tumbling backwards flat against the closet under the stairs.

A huge gray dog charged into the kitchen, its claws in desperate need of clipping as it slid across the floor and sounded like it slammed into the bottom cabinets..

I immediately threw up the best version of a protective wall I could—enchanting the hallway to look like a bare wall so the dog wouldn't come searching for me. No matter if it were a stray or not, the beast was huge enough to break through a door. That was reason enough to keep back.

My heart raced as I took a few steps forward, curious. What was it doing here? And how long had it been here?

It whined some more and I couldn't help but peek my head around the corner into the kitchen. Sure enough, the huge thing was shaking himself off from the collision with the cabinetry as he stood up. On all fours, he was easily three feet tall from the top of his head down. Great Dane, if I had to guess.

He lifted his head and peered right at me, obviously sensing me standing here through the enchantment. Darn it. I forgot to cast the rest of it—he was dog, of course he could hear and smell me.

What does one do when they find a stray in their house? I hadn't much experience with dogs in particular—Grandmother and my Aunties always had cats lying around everywhere but never dogs—and I wasn't sure if I should approach him or not. It looked like he was pretty used to the place, calm even.

Only one way to find out.

His ears stood up, twitching as I took in a deep breath and lowered the enchantment. I blinked, keeping my fingers crossed as I tried to decide whether it was best to stare him down to establish dominance or if that was stupid given the fact that we were strangers to one another.

He didn't seem to care one way or the other and ignored me to walk out to the backside of the veranda where I'd kept the screen door open for some breeze.

I followed him to the window, surprised to see the dog push open the outer screen door to go trotting outside to the back yard. This raggedy looking mutt seemed pretty capable of fending for himself at least. He was pretty skinny, but his eyes had been bright and silvery, so maybe he was just passing through the abandoned house looking for food?

"I'm definitely going to check this place for holes. Small and large alike, apparently."

No longer worried about the tall brute, I walked out the back door myself and shielded my eyes from the sun threatening to blind me over the tops of the live oaks in the backyard. The Spanish moss hung down from the limbs and swayed in time with the wind. It was a beautiful sight from my view.

Except for the rows of gravestones poking up out of the earth.

4
CURSED

"Oh no. Oh no, no, no."

I searched through my duffle bag for the file on the Hampton House that Gregory had given me. Throwing the screen door open I nearly tripped off the porch, stumbling over damaged bricks and more exposed roots as I went to investigate.

A few dozen gravestones of varying shapes and sizes, all in some kind of mossy disarray were looming at the edge of the property right by the trees. Behind the house was a side street that was just visible through the live oak's trunks, and how had I not known there was a darn cemetery here? On my property, from the looks of it!

The headstone closest to me looked like it may have been the newest addition to the lot, with its cleaner lines and less shabby state. I slowly picked my way through the overgrown grass, making the oddest mental note to search my spell book for the proper harm-free rodent remover when I got the chance. Rats were a problem in the house when I was a child, but I wasn't sure if that was still the case or not.

I wasn't the macabre type, though I've seen my share of it, but cemeteries were always a small interest of mine. The trouble with cemeteries though, was that they had quite a knack for being a haven for the midling spirits. Or the ghosts who haven't figured out they need to move on, in other words. They were few and far between, but an old haunt like this was sure to have a least one of those dead folks milling about without a clue that they were dead.

In fact… the hair on the back of my neck stood up more and more the closer I got to the cemetery. The small gate at the other end was hanging open, barely creaking in the breeze.

"I'll be darned if there ain't at least one of them here."

Coming up on the gravestone, I ran my hand along the smooth marble top of it, somewhat admiring the rounded edges. A bouquet of dead wildflowers lie on the ground in front of it, probably from the summer if I had to guess.

"Hazel Hampton. Loving wife, sister, friend. March 17th, 1961. December 24th, 2018. Oh my, that's terrible," I whispered to myself. To die on a day like that when everyone else is full of sentiment and cheer… I sighed, patting the top of it. "So sorry, sweetheart."

"Ha. She was hardly that."

I jerked my hand back and spun around. A woman with a stern mouth and sharp eyes was standing not ten feet from me, the scowl on her face sticking out above all else.

"I'm sorry?"

She nodded to the gravestone. "Hazel. Thought she was better than everyone else, you see. A sweetheart? More like a wretched neighbor."

I arched a brow at this woman, already conjuring up a judgment in my mind. Pushing it back, I offered her a polite enough smile.

"Well I'm sorry to hear that. Hopefully you won't find me as unsavory." I stuck out my hand. "I'm Birdie, your new neighbor."

She glanced down at my hand and pursed her lips even

harder. "I see. I hadn't realized someone had bought that old dump. No one ever tells me anything around here though, so I probably shouldn't be that surprised."

Obviously sizing me up, she reluctantly shook my hand. "Willa-Mae Hurst. I live right on the other side of the cemetery there." She pointed to a smaller house about a hundred yards back from the west end of the cemetery, decked out in random figures ranging from cats to what looked like garden gnomes.

Willa-Mae... this must be the woman Gregory warned me about. Apparently Miss Hurst was the neighborhood gossip and had a penchant for sticking her nose exactly where it didn't belong. I'd joked that there was one of 'em in every town I'd ever stayed in, but he didn't think it was that funny. He didn't tell me she was the next closest house, however. I'd have to bring her back up to him tomorrow night.

"It's a pleasure to meet you Miss Willa-Mae," I replied. Well, maybe pleasure was too strong of a word.

"Mm-hm. You said your name is Birdie? That's a strange name. Is it short for something?"

I shook my head, reciting the same words I've heard for over a century. "Birdie, and that's all. My mother fancied herself a naturalist. And birds were her favorite by far. Thus my name. At the very least, when someone calls out to me in a crowded room there's less confusion."

Willa-Mae didn't look too amused. "You got a last name?"

What a charmer she was. "Devaine."

Another curt nod and she placed her hands on her wide hips. "Devaine, huh? You must be new around here then. Probably what, fifty? Somewhere 'round there?"

The corner of my mouth quirked up. Even now it was rather rude to talk about a woman's age. It was ironic that she considered me new, though. "You could say I've got history with Nella. And sure. We'll go with fifty if that's what you think."

"Oh, you're one of those coy women. I don't do coy. What I say, I mean. And that's that."

"And that's good to know, Miss Willa-Mae. At least I know you'll always give me the honest truth."

She shifted her weight to one side, looking at me as if she didn't know where to place me just yet. "Hm. Well, if you want my honest truth... I think it was a mistake for you to buy that worn-down place," she said, jutting her thumb in the direction of my house. "If you're a God-fearing woman, you might even think the devil had something to do with building it. It's been a curse to the Hamptons for a long time, far as I know. You'd do well to watch your back."

"Watch my back?" I repeated. "That sounds an awful lot like a threat."

"Not exactly. I'm just sayin'. Every time the Hamptons would pass the place down to the next one in line, something odd happened. Be on your p's and q's, is what I mean. Or don't. I don't care one way or the other."

Oh my. And here I thought she was just an old lady with a mean streak. Nope. I had to get the superstitious one. Mind you, a lot of superstitions were that way for a reason... but still. I didn't need this woman running around telling people my place was haunted or cursed or whatever.

"Thank you for the advice," I finally said, keeping my tone neutral. I didn't want to sound patronizing—the last thing I wanted was to get on this woman's bad side from the get-go. A gossip was one thing. A menacing neighbor like her though, was something different for a witch like me.

She gave me another nod.

"I should probably get going. I've got a lot of work ahead of me as you can imagine." Including working on some boundary lines around my house. *I'll have to pick up a big bag of rock salt from the hardware store, too.*

Willa-Mae took a few steps back before turning on her heel and walking back past the rows of gravestones without another word to me.

"Such a lovely woman you are," I muttered under my breath. Watching my temper with her was important if I wanted to keep things peaceful between us.

Because one way or the other, I was going to have to be very careful around Willa-Mae Hurst. If she found out the truth about me, there was not a doubt in my mind that she would tell the whole world with glee.

5
WITCH HAZEL LANE

For an early fall night in Mississippi, it sure was chilly out last night. Cooler weather at the beginning of the season usually meant cooler heads prevailed during conflict, if you asked any witch worth her salt. And believe me, a smart witch never left home without a little pinch of the stuff somewhere.

After a long trip to the hardware store and the new Walmart in town, I'd managed to get the essentials I needed to make it through the first week or so.

I cleaned out the refrigerator which had definitely seen its fair share of gruesome, I wiped down everything in the kitchen, so I didn't feel quite so grimy putting my new set of dishes and silverware in the cabinets and drawers. I even set up the air mattress, as much as I missed sleeping on the luxurious pillow-top bed back in my penthouse in Vegas.

Before the end of the night, I was mainly stocked up and ready to get to work on fixing up my new humble abode. And I couldn't help but smile as I drifted off with that funny feeling of accomplishment settling in.

What I didn't expect was to be woken up by wet feet.

"Ugh! What in the Sam Hill!?" I shouted, scrambling

further up my air mattress until I rolled right off, thudding to the floor in a bleary mess.

At the other end stood that giraffe-legged mutt, drool hanging down from his mouth. He gave a sniff to the air and regarded me with big gray eyes.

"You did not," I growled, wiggling my toes with disgust as I realized yep, he sure did. "How in the world did you get back in here anyway? I thought I was rid of you yesterday!"

He licked at his chops and trotted over closer to me on the floor, sniffing me. I glared at him as I pulled myself back up and leaned down to wipe my feet.

"We're not playing this game. No sir. This is my house now, and you'll do well to remember it!" Why I was talking to this dog like he actually understood me, I had no idea.

But he let out a small growl before turning around and promptly running out of the room and down the hallway until I heard his heavy paws rushing down the staircase. And then there were the deep barks that felt like they rambled around in my chest—he had sensed something.

Sure enough, the doorbell rang, startling me. Guess the busted thing worked after all.

I glanced in the small mirror I'd hung by the closet. Oh no —this would not do at all.

I hurried to get dressed and run a brush through the nest on my head before I did my best not to get out of breath rushing down the steps. The doorbell rang one more time before I yanked the door open, my cheeks warm.

A woman with kind blue eyes stood in the doorway with a huge glass dish in her arms. "Good morning. You must be our new neighbor."

She wore a soft blue dress and had her dark brown hair done up and framing her face in a way that flattered her.

I smiled back at her. "Why yes, I am! I'm Birdie. Birdie Devaine. Just moved in yesterday, in fact."

"It's so nice to meet you, Birdie. My name's Geena. I live

over there across the way. Twenty-nine—with the red door." Over her shoulder I could see the pretty white house with its brick red door and a younger woman pulling a toddler along behind her as she walked over to one of the cars in the drive. A little boy stomped after them, not looking too happy.

"That's my daughter Ruby, and my grand babies Max and Eva. They're all a handful to be perfectly honest," she laughed, following my gaze. "Ruby usually takes the kids back home after Sunday school. It was Grammy weekend, as they like to call it."

"That's sweet. I bet they love that," I replied, pulling the door behind me as the dog's barking only got louder. Geena didn't seem to mind, though.

"I eat it up. Until they start getting cranky on me. Then I'm happy to hand them right back to Ruby and Shawn. Right after the luncheon, too."

I raised a brow. "Luncheon?"

She laughed, shaking her head. "Don't mind me, I'm a little addled on the weekends. I'm newly retired... Sometimes it feels like I'm past the days of explaining myself to people. No, no," she quickly added, seeing the apologetic look on my face. "No need to be sorry. It's my fault for assuming you knew what I meant. I help host the church's luncheon after the late service. I used to help with the breakfast after early service, but I figure I've been doing early service my whole life, so why not mix it up? Plus, I could use the extra hour of sleep after being on my feet for thirty-seven years." She added a wink and held up the glass dish covered in tinfoil.

"I nearly forgot why I came over here to begin with! We had some leftover green bean casserole from the luncheon, and I thought I'd swing by and introduce myself and offer you up some. If you'd like. It's a good recipe, though I'm somewhat biased." Geena flashed another grin at me.

Well, she was definitely an upgrade from Willa-Mae. "It

does smell rather good from where I'm standing," I admitted. "And I haven't exactly had the chance to get a full stock of food just yet. Thank you kindly for this, Miss Geena."

She snorted, surprising me as I took the casserole dish from her hands. "No need to be all formal around here, honey. All us girls are old friends and I'm pretty sure T.J. would pitch a fit if anyone referred to her as a Miss anything," she said, chuckling as I tilted my head.

"Oh. Are you... are you all friends in the neighborhood here?" I asked, genuinely curious. "It's been a while since I've been around the friendly type folk like that. Most neighbors come and go without so much as a hello nowadays."

"You know, I hear a lot of that. It's sad really, that things aren't the way they used to be. Where everyone got along just fine and knew everyone else. Ruby's neighborhood in the next town over is like that. She hardly knows a soul there, and they've lived there for over a year now. Witch Hazel Lane is a bit different. Most of us have been driving each other batty for forty some-odd years, believe it or not," she said with a wry smile.

The one thing I hadn't truly experienced—having girl-friends that lasted as long as I have. After my dearest friends from my younger days had all passed, I refused to keep others that closely. It was akin to losing a family member in my case.

I hesitated, realizing I was being rather rude by making her stand out here on the veranda. I cleared my throat and slipped my fingers into the door handle of the storm door, pulling it open as I precariously balanced the heavy dish in my arms. "Come on in, Geena."

She followed behind, helping me with the doors. "Whew. It's been a while since I've been in this place."

"Really?"

She nodded, this time not quite meeting my eyes. "My girlfriend Hazel lived here for most of her life, actually. The house was passed down in her family. She died last winter, though."

An ache spread through my chest for her. "I'm so sorry to hear that. I came across a newer headstone in the back. Hazel Hampton, was it?"

"Yep. That was Hazel. Her family wasn't very close to her anymore, aside from her husband of course. So we took it upon ourselves to all chip in and see to it that her memorial and funeral expenses were all covered. Poor Anthony couldn't handle all of it on his own."

"It must have been a very tough thing for him. Did she have any children?"

"No, it was just her and Anthony. She and Tull—T.J. that is—they didn't want any. It was one of the reasons why they got along so well. Anyway," she said, her voice distant. "Enough of all those sad memories!"

She followed me into the kitchen where I placed the dish in the refrigerator.

"Do you happen to know when the cemetery was put back there?" I finally asked after Geena gave me the run down on who lived where in the cul de sac.

She shrugged. "I'm not an expert on the house's history. Though I think it was after this was built and not before. Hazel told us the first grave belonged to Rudolf's youngest child when he caught pneumonia, I believe. Then the rest of them came after. Most of them Hamptons, though there are others."

Oh boy. A whole family worth of history right behind my house. I'm sure that won't be a problem *at all.*

"I see. I was just surprised to see it when I first got here."

She raised her brows. "Did you not know about it?"

I shook my head, feeling a little gullible if I were being honest. "It wasn't mentioned to me. Though to be fair, I was pretty adamant on hurrying the whole thing along. I um, didn't want to have to stay at the hotel in town or anything. Pricey."

It wasn't that she looked like she doubted me—more that she was trying to figure out more to my story. "Definitely. And you bought the house before you saw it?"

I winced. "Something like that. I know that probably sounds nuts."

Geena laughed and patted my hand. "I've heard stranger things, believe me. Are you one of those house flippers? There's this one show I love to trash talk on HGTV…"

I giggled. "I know just the one you're talking about, too. But I'm no house flipper. Too much of an investment just to turn around and sell it. I bought this place just to live in."

"It is a rather lovely place. Once you get past the fixing of it and all," she said, nodding as she looked up at the ceiling. "Though there's an awful lot of fixing needed, I bet."

"You're on the money there. I'm just hoping I'm not over my head."

It crossed my mind only then that the house had been oddly quiet. Where'd the dog run off to? Hopefully he didn't come bounding back into the kitchen. I was on the taller end for a woman, 5'9", while she was easily a good seven or eight inches shorter. That mutt would likely knock her right on her rear.

We chatted for a few more minutes, Geena giving me the rundown of where to find things in town. I humored her, but I was surprised to see that maybe things really had changed in Nella after all. I mean there was the Walmart now, anyway.

"I better get going," she finally said. "I volunteered to help Cinda get ready for a wedding order tomorrow. She runs the bakery downtown. And she's a maverick at it. She hates asking for help so I always make sure to offer it so she doesn't have to. After all, how else am I supposed to keep busy at night? I'm not too big on books, and the newspaper and news channels depress the heck out of me."

"I do some embroidery. It's nothing special though. And I doubt I'll have much time to with all this renovating."

"Oh really? I've always wanted to learn how to embroider. Maybe you could pop on over and teach me sometime!"

I smiled. "Sounds like a plan."

"Oh! I almost forgot," Geena said more so to herself than to me. "What's your phone number, Birdie?"

She pulled out her phone at the same time I did, both of us bursting into laughter. "I'm still not used to using my contact list here," she said, tapping through the menus on her phone. "But I can't exactly keep my address book on me all the time. It's thicker than this darn thing," she said, tilting her phone up toward me.

I nodded. She made a good point. "I know exactly what you mean. My manager wants me to text him whenever we need to chat. Says he hates talking on the phone. Well, isn't that what it's for?" I said, typing my name and number into her phone. She took mine from me and did the same.

"Exactly. Ruby says the same thing. Yet I distinctly recall having to boot her off the phone several times when we first got our computer set up when she was in high school. Whenever I'd try to log on and email someone, she was either staying up past her bedtime on the landline, thinking she was a sneaky thing, or on the stinkin' computer herself."

As she handed my phone back, I glanced down at it. Geena Marveaux. The last name sounded old like mine—like the French Huguenots that moved into this area back in the 1700s. But it didn't ring a bell.

"You should come on over and meet the rest of the girls. Are you free sometime this week?"

I froze. Now, I was all about making friends and playing well with others. But in light of the High-Order's recent public announcement, I wasn't sure I wanted the spotlight on me just yet.

"I don't know... I do have quite a lot of work ahead of me..."

She waved me off. "I swear we don't bite. Well, T.J. is a bit of wild card there, but we know how to muzzle her so I wouldn't worry about all that. It doesn't have to be a formal occasion or anything. Maybe just pop on over to my place in the early evening? Like I said, I'm retired from the hospital. Ruby goes to work around six, so you never know with her. But Francine closes up her chair at the salon at five during the week, and Cinda leaves The Macaroon Boutique around the same time. T.J. is likely to be at home downing one of her Coors Light around then, and if we can get her off her rear and away from her cats, then all the better."

Geena was awfully kind to invite me, especially since she didn't know much more than diddly squat about me. And I most certainly did not want to come off as rude to her. I could tell by the way she held herself that she was the leader of this group of friends and to rebuff her would probably not be a good start with meeting the rest of them.

I sighed, giving in. "I think I could find some time to stop by and chat for a little while anyway. I'll be sure to call you and make sure you're available."

The sunlight crawled across the bare floor of the sitting room, and I wiped at the sweat on my forehead. I'd been hard at work peeling back the old wallpaper around the room and even the bandana I'd wrapped around my head wasn't helping much. And of course it wasn't normal wallpaper—no that would've been too easy. It had to be the old Victorian-esque wallpaper that was pasted on cheesecloth material that had essentially bled into the wall.

By the time I took a look at my watch, I shook my head. "I cannot believe it's already been three hours. My stars, this is taking longer than I thought!"

I was hauling the scraps of debris into the garbage when I wheeled it outside, pulling a face at the stench of it, when I paused for a moment.

And then it hit me again. The feeling of being watched.

I spun around, eyeing the staircase, then the short hallway that led to the basement and the kitchen. Although I didn't see anything, I knew that didn't mean a thing. Picking my way over some of the debris I'd cleared out, I peeked into the kitchen. Still nothing.

The hair on the back of my neck stood up, just like when I was outside yesterday checking out the cemetery. Which only meant one thing.

I for sure had a spirit wanting to hang around.

"Sorry friend, but it's time to skedaddle out of here, wherever you are. Whomever you are," I said loudly, looking around the room. "And I just cleaned this floor. So keep your footprints off."

It took some doing, and I was missing a few of the usual requirements so I had to substitute some things... but I had my ready-made spirit ditch supplies lying out on the kitchen counter. If I was going to do this, then I needed to do it now and do it well.

The last time I had to help guide a spirit on, I had just gotten engaged to my third husband. Go figure that the moment Ronnie got his camper, we stumbled across the spirit of a dead hiker in the Smokies. I swore that was the last time I'd do it and here I was again, having to prep for the unpleasant act.

Behind me there was the tell-tale sniffing of the Great Dane coming from the servant's staircase. I glanced over my shoulder, frowning.

"You know, you have some lousy timing there. And how

in the heck do you keep getting in here? Keep it up and I'm going to have to charge you rent. Now you stay put so I can get this all sorted outside."

I was well aware that it was only four in the afternoon, but I wasn't about to wait until the witching hour, much less the thinning of the veil at three AM, so it needed to be handled now. I only had so much patience for spirits creeping in on me like that, regardless of the type.

I gathered everything in my now empty duffel bag and dragged everything outside, laying it all back out around me in what I determined to be the middle of the cemetery. The gate creaked as I knelt down, but the wind had died down.

I sighed. I didn't want to halfway attempt it, so I took a minute to meditate and clear my mind.

Spreading out the circle of rock salt around me, I chanted under my breath. "Cleanse and consecrate this space."

The energy around me was starting to press against the barrier of the salt circle—invisible to the naked eye but easy enough to sense.

The candles were lit, the spell book was at my feet, and I'd begun the enchantment, trying to pull in the interest of the spirit. Concentrating on the energy, I reached out with my mind the best I could, searching for the spirit. "Come to me, it is time to move on. Come to me, I will guide you to the great beyond," I called out in a low voice, picking up the fat white pillar candle and watching the flame flicker in front of me. I waved it around, turning in circles as I continued the chant.

Out of the corner of my eye something glittered on the other side of the cemetery, reflecting the sunlight behind me. I froze.

Willa-Mae was standing at the edge of her property, phone in hand and most definitely recording me as I now stood with the spirit's energy swirling around me in a glittering whirl. There was no doubt she could see something going on, and I must have looked insane standing inside the salt circle, chanting and waving the candles all about.

Reality slapped me right in the kisser. I blinked, trying to make sense of it. The bottom of my stomach seemed to disappear as I stood there afraid to move.

I just got here. I sank all of my money into this place—I can't very well leave. I haven't even finished buying curtains for all of the windows yet...

Across the way, Willa-Mae stared at me with an arrogant, smug grin.

I was not going to run this time.

6
THE GRIFTER

The only thing I could think to do was throw up the best darn screen I'd ever come up with. Except it was easier said than done, doing it on the fly. It was one thing to have a whole show choreographed and planned ahead of time—it was quite another thing to be on the verge of panic and throwing something together.

I nearly tripped over my own two feet trying to pick up the candles and blow them out. I could still see Willa-Mae out of the corner of my eye, and she was taking cautious steps forward from behind one of the tall gravestones.

"Shoot, shoot, shoot!" I whispered hoarsely, doing my best to grab everything and throw it into the duffel bag. I wracked my brain for the perfect screen, but my mind was drawing a blank.

Get ahold of yourself old girl. How can I turn this around...?

Drawing in a deep breath I concentrated on the wall of space in front of Willa-Mae... And envisioned it as pure energy—a vibrating and wavering force of energy. I pictured it warping into what I wanted it to look like, one detail at a time.

Willa-Mae's eyes were unfocused, blinking up at the

space before her. She screwed up her face as she tilted her head back to look at the sky.

A light breeze picking up and a small raindrop hitting her cheek. Then dark, heavy clouds bursting with torrents of rain rolling across the sky all at once. Releasing rain by the buckets, and hail too.

She screeched, wrapping her cardigan tightly around herself as she imagined the image I conjured in my own mind.

Gusts of wind strong enough to snap the branches above her head like toothpicks.

There was another screech, this time, she was ducking back out of the cemetery as fast as she could. In her imaginary conundrum, she clutched her phone to her chest.

I frowned. She wasn't walking out of my sight with that thing if I had any say.

I noticed the cardigan she had wrapped around her didn't appear to have any pockets, so I imagined there was one perfectly sized to store her phone. The moment she thought to put the phone into a pocket that didn't exist, it dropped to the ground and Willa-Mae ran back to her house without another look backward.

Now would've been a perfect time to have Corinne on my side ready to do damage control.

Willa-Mae's screen door slammed shut, and I carried on my screen magic for a minute, just in case she decided to peek through her blinds at the supposed storm.

Satisfied that she wasn't looking, I hurried over to where she dropped her phone in the grass and snatched it up before hauling my tailpiece back inside. The guiding on would just have to wait.

Luckily for me, Willa-Mae wasn't too protective of her phone to have a password on it and I was able to locate the short clip she'd begun to record of me out in the cemetery.

"Bye-bye and good riddance," I said, shaking my head as I

tapped the little red trashcan in the corner of the screen. "And maybe if I'm really lucky, she'll just forget the whole thing ever happened."

My nerves were shot for the day. I poured myself a sizable glass of my favorite cabernet and went to lie down on my air mattress. It wasn't my favorite chaise lounge by the gas fireplace, but it would do for now.

For the third time in a row, I tried to screw the last of the lightbulbs into the candelabra over where I would eventually have an elegant dining room table.

Getting this part of the house renovation done wasn't something I was truly worried about. I first learned about electrical wirings and workings back when they were just becoming the standard in residences. A friend of mine was kind enough to teach me while he worked at the electric company and I had a job as a seamstress. Back then I was like a sponge soaking up all the knowledge I could and was eager to learn.

But trying to adjust the different colored wires coming out of the light switch required more of me. Four whole YouTube tutorial videos later and I was about as close to being an electrician as I could be. For now. I was definitely going to need a professional to help with the heavy-duty stuff, however.

With the last lightbulb in place, I eased myself down the step ladder and flipped the switch. All twelve lights burned bright and warm, and I stood back smiling to myself. Not too shabby after all.

"You've still got it," I muttered to myself, turning the lights back off. Well, that was one project scratched off the ever-growing list.

I went to wash my hands after getting them covered in

dust and goodness knows what else, and nearly tripped over the tarp that I had lying on the ground. *I swear this place is like a construction zone.*

I washed up, then decided mid-way that I would sweep the kitchen... promptly forgetting that I did not, in fact, own a broom. Just another thing to add to that darn list.

If I had paid attention to my transfiguring lessons when I was a child, I might be able to cobble one together out of things I did have. But the last time I'd pulled that off was when I ran away from Nella all those years ago.

I was in desperate need of a blanket at the first inn I'd found after hoofing it northward for a couple of days. It turned out to be a ratty blanket, but I was pretty good with the needle and thread and managed to fix it into something a little less drab once I'd scraped up enough for the sewing materials and a couple days' worth of food.

In fact, the shabby thing was folded neatly in the bottom of my suitcase—a reminder of where I started. While Grandmother was strict and not at all the nostalgic type, she was keen on teaching me the value of remembering which garden you grew from.

Shaking myself from my memories, I sat down on the step that led from the foyer to the sitting room. "Birdie, girl. You're due for some proper furniture—your body needs something a little more cushiony to rest on. And this step ain't cutting it," I said, sighing.

The doorbell's chime went off barely ten feet from me and I jumped, my heart racing. I blinked, letting the shock wear off before I pulled myself to my feet. Recognition hit me like a bolt of lightning. How could I forget about Gregory stopping by this evening?

There were no curtains at the windows surrounding the door just yet, so I had no trouble at all seeing that it was in fact, Gregory.

"Gregory! Thank you for stopping by. I appreciate it," I said through the screen door. "Won't you come in?"

He nodded and swept his hair back from his forehead awkwardly. "Of course."

I led him into the kitchen where we could at least stand at the island and finish sorting everything out. My cheeks burned as I realized how utterly vacant my house still looked. Now, now. There's plenty of time to get cleaned up.

Gregory placed the thick file down on the countertop, followed by a plastic container that looked just large enough to fit one of my Grandmother's sponge cakes inside.

He patted the top of it. "And I brought this, too." Opening the lid, he grinned. "A homemade Bundt cake. Think of it as a house-warming gift."

My eyes went wide. "Oh? My, that's awfully kind of you dear. I didn't take you for the baking type!"

He chuckled but cleared his throat, looking a little embarrassed about the whole thing. Well darn, I hadn't meant to make him feel bad.

"But thank you so much. I can't even recall the last time someone's baked something for me." I leaned over the Bundt cake, catching mighty strong whiff of alcohol as I did. Pulling back, I laughed. "Is this a rum cake? I'd hold back on pouring the whole bottle in next time."

Gregory nodded. "Oh, uh, sorry about that. My girlfriend gave me the idea. She's always cooking with the stuff. Not that she's an alcoholic or anything!" He quickly added, his cheeks burning red under his closely cropped beard. "Anyway. I try to make my clients feel right at home," he said, his eyes following the dingy cabinetry around the room. "Especially when you're really just starting out."

He had a point. I couldn't really refuse such a sweet gesture—even if it did smell like a whole bottle of Captain Morgan's. "Of course. And it really was sweet of you; most realtors drop off the keys and skedaddle out as soon as they can unload the house on the buyers."

"I'm not most realtors," he said with the quirk of his mouth. He pulled out a pen and tapped it to the file on the counter. "I've got everything here, ready to be signed. Are you ready to be the official owner of this dump? Sorry," he chuckled, shaking his head. "That was rude of me. I apologize."

I shrugged. "Well, you aren't wrong. It's got good bones though, so I think I can turn it around. All hope isn't yet lost here."

Gregory wiped at his brow. "Very true."

It didn't take as long as I figured it would to fill everything out. I signed and initialed every blank space and addendum, finishing the very last signature with a flourish and a small smile.

I sorted the paperwork into a neat stack and tapped the bottom before sliding the whole thing back into the manila file he'd handed me. The smile on my face grew even wider. "All finished!"

"Good, good. I uh, think that's it, Miss Devaine. We'll get the deed properly recorded on our end, and you should be all good to go from here. Did you have any other questions?"

I shook my head. "No, sir. I believe you've covered everything."

Gregory smoothed down his tie, giving me a funny smile. "Great. Perfect. I'll just take this here file and I'll be out of your hair. You can always call the office if you need anything. But hopefully everything about your renovation project will go well and you won't need any help from us."

We shook hands and I walked him to the front door. "Thank you so much for everything, dear," I said, patting him on the shoulder. "I appreciate you bending the rules for me a little bit to help get me in here."

Gregory waved me off with a chuckle. "No need to worry

about any of that. It was just pushing the auction paperwork back a little bit so we could squeeze the sale in before. How could I turn down someone from their dream?" he said, quoting something I'd said at our first meeting.

I nodded. "Well, I appreciate it nonetheless. Have a good evening, all right? And drive careful, dear."

And with that, he was out the door and I was facing the inside of my new house. Everything was official—there was no going back now.

"Now I just need some wine to celebrate."

Heading into the kitchen, I stopped dead in my tracks. The Great Dane had returned, and this time was nearly upright against the counter, trying to make off with Gregory's rum cake.

"Shoo! Get away from there you big ol' grifter. You sure know how to make a quiet entrance, don't you? You must fancy yourself a ninja of sorts, slipping in here without a peep." I was comfortable enough to nudge him away from the food, shaking my head. "One of these days I'm going to catch you sneaking in. And that'll be the last of your squatter days, buster."

He whined at me as I picked up the cake, and I could've sworn his big gray eyes were tearing up. Maybe it was just a trick of the light.

"Stop that," I said, sighing. "I don't have the time nor patience to be worrying about another mouth to feed. There's a reason I never had children, you know. Oh, listen to me," I groaned. "Talking to you like you're going to say something back..." I raised an eyebrow, waiting. "All right, I was just checking. I've never heard of a talking animal aside from that ridiculous parrot my Auntie Lilian had. What a nuisance that thing was!"

I was still talking to the dog, but I figured at that point what was the harm in it? It was nice to have someone... or something... to talk to at any rate.

My stomach grumbled as if it agreed with the dog's whining. I guess there's nothing left to do but eat some dinner.

I studied the dog for a moment before glancing down at the rum cake still in my hands. It probably wasn't a good idea for a dog to eat cake, so I fished out some of the deli meat from the fridge and tossed it over to him. The meat barely touched the ground before he snapped it right up.

I chuckled and grabbed a fork from the silverware drawer. "Bon appetite, I guess," I mumbled, looking down at the rum cake in the plastic container.

It was odd. The cake had smelled so strong earlier when Gregory brought it over. Now it smelled like... like regular pound cake. The first few bites were much the same. Not at all strong like I thought they'd be. In fact, I couldn't really taste the rum in the cake.

I sniffed. "Must be these blasted allergies. I'll have to brew some chamomile and honey tea. And probably pick up some medicine from the store while I'm at it."

The dog made an appreciative noise and circled around a few times before collapsing in a great big heap in front of the breakfast nook.

The cake was pretty plain, not in a bad way, but in a surprising way.

"I've got it!" I said, realizing I'd been staring at the dog who was starting to twitch in his sleep. He opened one lazy eye and looked at me before returning to his snoozing.

"Grifter. That's what I'll call you. You're always in here skulking about anyway, so I might as well. Do you like it?"

I scooped up another bite of the no-rum cake, savoring the sweetness. Grifter stared at me almost as if he knew there was no chance in Hades that I would let him have a slice.

I pointed the spoon at him, smiling—perhaps a little smugly. "You know what? It doesn't even matter—I like it. I think it suits you."

Grifter flopped back down with his eyes closed, his heavy jowls quivering as he let out a huge sigh. Dogs, I swear.

I knew it was silly, but I couldn't help but reach down to scratch behind his ears before I finished cleaning up the kitchen.

"Oh my word," I said, turning the shower head off. The shower was supposed to help my aching muscles after the work I'd been up to, but it didn't seem to keep away the chills that raked up and down my spine. It was a cooler night than most this time of year, but I was surprised to feel the cold clinging to my bones more than usual. Wrapping a towel around myself didn't seem to help one bit.

"I better put together some elderberry syrup in the morning. I do not want to get sick," I muttered to myself as I got ready for bed. I pulled my covers around tightly.

I wasn't too deep into a dream where Brad Pitt was about to whisk me away on his private yacht when I awoke with a start. Staring blearily at the window, my eyes adjusted to the dark room. The air was eerily still. How long had I been asleep? Without an alarm clock, I sleepily reached for my cell phone charging by the bed. 3:25 AM.

A high-pitched screech echoed through the air just as I pulled my covers back over myself, and I jumped up out of bed, rattled. *It's coming from outside...*

I threw open one of the big windows and tried to see around the corner of the house—the scream was most certainly coming from somewhere behind it.

My room was barren of anything useful I'd need to defend myself, which meant I could only rely on my wits and my magic. Usually it was enough to suffice but something about that scream had me carefully tying my robe and tiptoeing cautiously downstairs.

The sound of an ambulance pierced through the night not far off before I'd made it all the way into the street. Somewhere someone was sobbing loudly.

I pulled my robe tighter, determined to figure out what in the name of buttered biscuits was going on. People were starting to peek out their bedroom windows along the street, a few of them even daring to step outside and take a look too.

I rounded the corner of my house. My stomach was knotting up as I picked my way through the grass. Early twilight mist clung to my bare feet.

The flashing lights of the ambulance caught my eye coming into the cul de sac. Several squad cars pulled up all around it, with cops piling out of them and rushing across the edge of my property where a small smattering of trees cut my yard off from Willa-Mae's side yard. They were headed toward the far side of the cemetery, to the side street.

"Oh my word," I whispered softly. Whatever was going on, it was not good.

I was desperate to know just what the heck was going on, so I veered around the gravestones and tried to sneak behind the tallest one to get a better look.

The police were busy taping off an area and some of them were huddled off to the side, radioing back to the office if I had to guess. The looks on their faces had a sort of matching grimness to them.

On the ground about twenty feet away from them, was a crumpled heap. I could just make out a bit of fabric—brightly patterned pants to go with the bright flip-flops I'd seen earlier today…

It felt as though my stomach had bottomed out.

The white sheet was being pulled over Willa-Mae's body just as I resisted the urge to retch.

7

IDLE HANDS

I must have been standing in the yard with my mouth wide open for a solid five minutes. If I wasn't careful, I was going to swallow some kind of flying unpleasantness.

Out of the corner of my eye I noticed someone slowly approaching from the now taped-off crime scene. Judging by the clean-pressed uniform despite the time of night, and the hat he was donning, the tall man was possibly the town's sheriff.

He cleared his throat when he was close enough for me to hear him. "You're the new owner of the Hampton House?" he asked me, nodding his chin toward the house behind me.

I turned and nodded, a chill running up my spine. I wrapped my robe around myself even tighter. "I am."

"And I'm Sheriff Paine," he said, studying me closely as he gave me an opening.

"Oh! It's nice to meet you, Sheriff. I'm Birdie Devaine."

"Well Miss Devaine, I'm sorry to report that your neighbor, Willa-Mae, was just found on the cemetery's property. Dead, God rest her soul. There may be potential foul play at hand. You own it, correct? The cemetery?"

I didn't very much like the way he kept referring to *'you.'* The other officers were all talking quietly amongst themselves, but I was able to pick up bits here and there. It sounded as though someone might have strangled the woman. She may have been ugly with me earlier, but I certainly wouldn't wish such a thing upon her. And I knew a thing or two about curses.

"I only met her the day before yesterday... what a horrible thing to happen to her! And you think someone might have murdered her?" I shuddered at the thought. With all the death I'd seen in my time, murder was a different creature.

"Pending the autopsy. She has no family, so we're not sure if we'll get the okay from the hospital's board to perform it, but hopefully we can. That means we find the possible killer faster."

"I just can't believe someone would do this..." my voice trailed off as I looked past Sheriff Paine to Willa-Mae's house. She was a liability to me anyway, sorry to say, but what if she had some dirt on someone else? She was apparently a big enough gossip for that to be feasible.

He was paying very close attention to me even as I let my mind wander some. "Seeing as it's practically the middle of the night, I'm sure you're wanting to head back to bed. All I ask is that you make the time to come into our office downtown in the morning so you can maybe help us. Can you do that for me, ma'am?"

No need to panic, Birdie girl. It's just because you're the closest neighbor and poor Willa Mae was technically found in your yard. They're just covering all their bases...

I cleared my throat. "Of course, Sheriff. Whatever I can do to help." Was I a fan of having to go down to the sheriff's office and answer questions after the business with Willa-Mae yesterday afternoon? Heck no. Did I really have a choice, though?

He tipped his hat, making it nearly impossible to see his

face. "No need to lose sleep worrying about it. We'll be out here all night anyway, so you'll be perfectly safe tonight."

I thanked him before he walked back over to the small group of officers standing over Willa-Mae's body. Another chill crawled its way up my spine.

The cell phone that was currently lying on my kitchen island was the kind of evidence the sheriff department would be on the lookout for. How in the world was I going to sneak that thing back over to Willa-Mae's house with a whole crime scene between everything?

I made sure to get up bright and early, even without a cup of Corinne's delicious crack of dawn cold brew to raise the dead. She would always make sure that it was ready for me as soon as I woke up at eight o'clock sharp. All I could think about was how much I missed my only real friend.

It was essential to come prepared for this so-called talk with the sheriff's department. I had to look as innocent as possible. Not that I wasn't innocent, but I didn't need Sheriff Paine and his crew sniffing around in my business, all things considered. I went with a pair of my favorite cropped pants and a light sweater, and even grabbed my most non-descript purse. It was a blend-in kind of affair.

Thinking that I might get out the door without much fanfare from the neighborhood, I stepped outside and locked up behind myself, only to find that I was dead wrong. Half the neighbors seemed to be out in the cul de sac, including Geena and her group of friends.

I bit my lip. Now, I wasn't someone who'd ever had much in the way of friends. Especially since I was always on the move, and I hadn't had much of a kinship with my family enough to want to stick my neck out for others. But I had to admit… a pang of shame hit me as I walked down my front steps.

To think that I could have been a part of something like that was nice. Given the wary looks on the women's faces now though, I didn't stand a snowball's chance in Hades at it. Even Geena looked concerned as I yanked my car door open.

The Nella sheriff's department was downtown, set not far from Saint Peter's Church—the pinnacle of Nella. The church's ivory spires reached way up and cast a shadow over most of the smaller buildings below it, including the one-story brick building I was walking into.

The inside of the Sheriff's office was dated, with that type of pine look that went out some time in the eighties. You could tell that this place used to be full of officers sitting at their desks smoking over stale coffees, just from the smell of it. I sighed and walked up to the reception desk.

"Excuse me. I believe Sheriff Paine is expecting me?"

The man behind the desk quickly wiped the crumbs off of his uniform and adjusted his thick coke-bottle glasses. "Your name, please?" he asked. The deep voice used was definitely not his natural tone.

Suppressing the urge to laugh, I gave it to him and thanked him as he directed me back to an empty room. I don't know what I'd imagined the inside of a police interrogation room to look like, but this was pretty close.

The walls were bare, save a couple of posters about saying no to drugs. The wood table looked like someone picked it up at a yard sale, and neither of the two chairs matched it. The only thing missing was one of those two-way mirrors.

The door creaked open and in came the sheriff. His demeanor was somewhat better as he took a seat opposite of me. "Ms. Devaine. Glad to see you. Thank you for taking time out of your morning to come have a chat with me."

I nodded. "I'd say I'm glad to be here, but that would be a lie. Of course I wish the circumstances were different."

His mustache twitched as he set a small black voice recorder on the table between us. "As do I. We don't usually get this kind of call in Nella." He waited a beat and turned the recorder on, aiming it toward me. "I'll just be asking you some questions to kind of help us get a picture of what was going on leading up to when Ms. Hurst's body was found. This here will be recording the conversation. Do you acknowledge that the answers you give are truthful and given under full and willing disclosure?"

"Yes, I do." Even still, a knot formed in my stomach.

"All righty. Let's start with the basics. Can you state your name and address for me?"

"Birdie Devaine, and I live at 29 Witch Hazel Lane, Nella, Mississippi."

"And how long have you lived in Nella, Ms. Devaine?"

That was really up for debate, but I gave him the simple answer. "I moved into the Hampton House the day before yesterday."

"What brought you to Nella, if you don't mind me asking?"

Something gnawed at me. Why was he asking something like that? Wasn't he supposed to ask me if I'd seen or heard anything last night?

I cleared my throat. "I just needed a change of pace. I heard Nella was a nice place to settle down."

"I'd like to think so," he replied, nodding. "Though it looks like we need to work on the peace and quiet. Moving on now… did you know the victim?"

"I wouldn't really say I knew her. I did meet her the day I moved in. She saw me walking around my yard and came over to introduce herself."

"And did Ms. Hurst seem coherent to you?"

I frowned. "Coherent?"

"We're looking for signs of distress, I mean to say. Did she seem particularly distressed when speaking to you at first?"

I shook my head. How was I supposed to know that? "No, that wasn't the impression I got from her."

"Oh? And what was your impression?"

"Ms. Hurst was... just curious about me, I suppose."

"How so?" He leaned back in his chair and regarded me carefully.

Why did it suddenly feel so stuffy in the room?

"She wanted to meet me of course, as I assume she wanted to know about the person who just moved in next door to her. And... she was surprised that I bought the place."

"The Hampton House is well-known to the town. Curiosity is natural in this situation I would think. Did Ms. Hurst say anything was troubling her that day?"

"No, she didn't." I went on to briefly explain the short conversation we'd had.

"Hm," Sheriff Paine said, tapping his finger to the file he'd brought in with him. "She told you the place was haunted."

I nodded. "She seemed very... wary of the house, I'd say. I understand it being a little off-putting with the cemetery there and all."

"It's like I said, Ms. Devaine. The Hampton House is well-known here. I'm not a superstitious man at all, but there are plenty in town who are. It doesn't sound like she was acting unlike herself, though."

"You were friends with her?" I asked, realizing that wasn't really what this conversation was for.

But he obliged anyway. "Acquaintances, more like. If you work here at the station, then you know her. She was... a frequent visitor. Not for any criminal activity, mind you. Ms. Hurst just had a way of... being particularly aware of everything going on. She fancied herself a sort of spy on behalf of us."

That did not surprise me in the slightest, but I kept my mouth shut.

"You last spoke with her at that time, correct? You didn't see or speak to Ms. Hurst afterward?"

This was the part I was not looking forward to. I hated a liar, and I most certainly couldn't tell Sheriff Paine that Willa-Mae caught me performing a guiding on. I had to choose my words carefully.

"I saw her yesterday. I was in my backyard again and I saw her… in her yard. She didn't say anything to me, though." None of what I said was untrue, at least. I did see her in her yard… once I'd thrown up that screen magic and she thought she was outrunning a sudden storm.

"What was she doing? Do you recall seeing anyone else with her?"

"I don't really know what she was doing. She wasn't out there for very long. And no, sir. I didn't see anyone else there with her." I wasn't exactly going to count the spirit I was trying to get rid of.

"What time did you last see her?"

"Ah… I'd say three o'clock."

"Could you describe to me what the rest of your day was like, Ms. Devaine? We just want to get a clearer picture of everything around the area leading up to her death."

My throat was dry as I went on to explain working on stripping the rest of the wallpaper, how Geena had stopped by and how Gregory had come over to help me finish the paperwork for the house.

"Once he left, I ate my dinner, took a shower and went right to bed. I was rather tired after all that work. Who knew renovating could be such hard work!"

He nodded slowly, his eyes narrowing ever so slightly. "Too true. I imagine it's a lot of work for one person."

Shrugging, I tried to play off the nervousness in my voice. "I like the hard work. It keeps me busy. My grandmother was always going on about idle hands being the devil's playground."

"Idle hands... Whatever the case, someone certainly had busy hands when they choked the life out of Ms. Hurst."

I bristled, not expecting something so forward coming from him. "That's terrible. A terrible thing to happen..." I said softly.

"No need to worry, Ms. Devaine. We're still gathering evidence for the case. Sooner or later, and I'm betting on sooner, we'll know more about who we're dealing with."

Evidence. I was technically innocent, but a blanket of heavy worry still covered me. Willa-Mae's phone was like a rattlesnake waiting to strike. I'd gotten rid of the *evidence* of me and my power from the phone, but I still hadn't figured out a way to sneak the darn thing back into Willa-Mae's house. It would hang over my head until it was taken care of —that I knew for sure.

"Well, Miss Devaine, I do believe that's all I have for you. We'll do some checking around, just to help support your whereabouts." Sheriff Paine pulled out a card and slid it toward me. "Here's my number if you suddenly remember something that could be useful to us. Anything at all."

Placing it into my purse, I tried to slap on a smile that hid the anxiety rising in my throat. "Yes, sir. I will do just that."

He pulled out his chair and stood as I did, nodding. "I'll have Parker at the front get your information. Again, thank you for stopping by."

The sheriff escorted me out of the room and said one more goodbye before heading down a different hallway and out of sight. I made my way back up front and lingered at the front desk, disappointed to see that the young man—Parker, apparently—was nowhere to be found.

I stood at the front, growing incredibly impatient. At the very least someone else could come get my information and let me leave.

Coming from down the same hall I had just left, a slightly

familiar face peeked at me from over a tall cardboard file box, I didn't really know her, but I did know who she was.

She had that same look of recognition on her face as if she knew of me too. "Oh! Sorry about that," she said, setting the heavy looking box on top of the reception counter. "Whew. These things are usually pretty light. You're my mama's new neighbor, right? The one who moved into the Hampton's house?"

So she did know who I was. "I sure am. I'm Birdie. And you must be Geena's daughter! I apologize, I don't quite remember your name." I was usually much better about things like that, but to be fair, Geena had caught me off guard.

She beamed at me. "Ruby Malveaux-Camden. I grew up on Witch Hazel Lane, but I'm sure Mama's told you that. It's lovely to finally meet you, Miss Birdie."

I waved her off. "No need for the formalities. Birdie will do just fine. Do you … work here?"

Ruby patted the top of the file box and sighed. "I'm the property and evidence clerk." She leaned in with a conspiratorial smile on her face, reminding me very much of her mother. "I'm hoping to start my own business soon, though. Then I can kiss the dusty evidence room goodbye."

I grinned at her cheekiness. "Sounds like you've got some plans in order, then," I said quietly.

"What are you doing here, anyway? Oh, I plum forgot. I don't know how though, considering it's all everyone's talking about around here."

I swallowed against the lump in my throat, glancing around the room. "What's that?"

"Willa-Mae. The woman they found by the Hampton's graves. You knew about that, didn't you?"

I nodded. "Unfortunately. Sheriff Paine had me come in for questioning."

Ruby chewed at her lip for a moment, before frowning.

"He's a good man. Sometimes a little on the skeptical side. I hope he wasn't harsh on you."

"No, no. Not at all. I understand he's just doing his job. And I'm happy to help—it's terrible what happened to Willa-Mae. I didn't hardly know her, but no one deserves that kind fate."

She nodded with me. "Definitely not. Willa-Mae didn't exactly get along with anyone, but she mostly kept to herself and didn't cause a lot of problems. Well… there was that one time at bingo night. She was an avid bingo player, and she nearly got in a fistfight with one of the orderlies that work at the hospital. She was fiercely competitive."

I raised a brow at this. "Hm. She must have been."

Ruby grunted as she went to pick up the box again. "I better get this back to my desk if I want a decent lunch break later. It was a pleasure meeting you Miss Birdie. Sorry—Birdie! Mama's always drilled manners in my head."

I smiled. "She seems like a good woman, your mama. And it was lovely to meet you too, Ruby. Hopefully I'll see you around the neighborhood."

"Of course! Maybe some time I can invite you over for supper. Once I get furniture, that is."

She laughed and went on her way, struggling under the weight of the file box. I stood there for another few minutes waiting for the young man to show back up and let me off the hook. Spending another minute here was likely to give me hives.

The phone rang at the reception desk, startling me from my thoughts. I glanced around to see if anyone was going to pick it up, but no one seemed to really care. This was one of those times I wish they had a bell to ring.

The caller must have finally given up and the phone shut up, though I was starting to pick up on another conversation. Two officers were standing behind me by the flags on the wall, their voices low.

"I don't know if I buy it. It's like where did they all come from, you know?"

The other officer scoffed. "Who cares? If they're real then we got a problem. I don't want no weirdos hanging around my family. We don't know what they're capable of yet."

"I guess not. It kind of reminds me of that comic book with the mutants. Freaks with powers and all that stuff. They weren't always good, but they weren't always bad."

"I don't care if they're good, bad, green, or covered in warts. These witches better stay away from me and mine if they know what's good for them."

I blinked and tried to remain perfectly still. The last time I heard a threat from a man in charge like that, he had made good on his promise and Grandmother ended up blind in one eye.

Luckily for me, the young man at the front desk finally showed back up. "Oh, you didn't have to hang around, ma'am. You're free to go."

I clutched my purse tightly and nodded before breezing past the officers who paid no mind to me. People were only scared of what they didn't understand. It was where most fear was based.

But my fear was that I already knew what happened when people turn on one another.

8
BETWEEN THE CUSHIONS

It was rather satisfying, seeing the pantry fully stocked for the first time. I had to budget carefully for everything, using coupons and the sales paper for bargains, but it paid off in the end. Everything was tucked away nicely in its own space. I even managed to find some sundries, a tea kettle, a few pots and pans, and a cheap porcelain set for my flour and sugar. I smiled as I filled up flour and sugar and set them on the countertop.

"Aren't you the little homemaker?" I said to myself, drumming my fingers on the island. "Though I could do with a cute valance over the kitchen window… I'll have to add that to the list, I suppose."

Anything I could do to keep what happened to Willa-Mae off my mind was welcome. Even though I could take care of myself, I was still uneasy about the idea of a cold-blooded killer lurking around my yard. Last night I hardly slept a wink.

The tea kettle on the stove started whistling and I tended to it, adding the boiling water to the tincture in the pot. Truthfully I should have done it last night, but at least with my oil I'd get some decent sleep tonight. The smell of cardamom pods and lavender oil wafted in the air after a minute or so, and I took the mixture off to sit and cool.

It was an old recipe that had been passed down through generations of the Devaine family, mother to daughter. Or grandmother to daughter in my case— my mother and father died when I was very young. I didn't know much about them since Grandmother never talked about them. And I didn't dare try to broach the subject myself.

The only thing I knew was thanks to those cows I called my Aunties, and that was that my father was not a warlock and he worked in the same textile mill that helped to create the very house I was now standing in.

I took my new broom and finally swept the dust and dirt off the kitchen tile and out the back door. Working my way around the veranda, I finished sweeping. As a special little surprise, I'd picked up a few large bones for Grifter, and I pulled one of them out of the bag on the counter inside and brought it back out to toss over to Grifter.

He sniffed at it hopefully, whined, and stalked off to go laze out in the sunshine.

I frowned. "For such a big ol' thing, you sure don't like to eat." I tried to feed him, even going as far as washing out an old bowl that was left behind and filling it with some kibble I'd picked up. But the kibble had stayed there for a couple of days, untouched.

I came to the conclusion that Grifter probably got his food from outside the house. I pushed open the screen door. "You're more stubborn than my ex! And I'm not talking about Cecil or Ronnie! That's right—I mean the devil himself. Richard. And that's saying something," I yelled out to him. There wasn't anyone close enough to really hear me anymore, so what did it matter?

I noticed for the first time in a couple of days that the cemetery was empty. No more officers walking by, taking pictures, walking the path between my house and Willa-

Mae's. It didn't even look like anyone was stationed over at her house anymore.

I bit my lip. Was it finally time?

After worrying over her phone, I came up with a plan to sneak it back into the house. It was very simple really, but I needed the time to think and not be distracted by the sheriff's department.

All I would need was to sneak past the officers without drawing their attention. My magical screens only worked so well—I could only realistically manipulate a screen with real people and real things that existed. I could project a torrential rainstorm and have the person under the enchantment truly feel as though they were getting rained on, but I couldn't make that person believe they were flying across the sky on a pink unicorn.

If I managed to make it past them, then I could use my skeleton key and jimmy it into the front door to unlock it. It was one of the only magical items I took with me when I ran away from home at fifteen. And boy had it come in handy since.

Running back inside to check out the front door, I saw that the entire cul de sac appeared empty. Most folks were probably at work. It was the perfect time, and I didn't want to have the phone in my house a minute longer.

Wiping the fingerprints from it was easy, and I kept it in a paper towel and stuck it in my back pocket before heading out to the backyard. The shadows cast by the live oaks between our houses covered up a good bit of the cemetery. I ignored the chill spreading across my skin and slipped undetected past the tallest headstones, making sure no one could see.

The trick was getting to the front door. There was a neighbor out cutting his grass a few houses down, but he was paying me no mind as I did my best to casually walk up the steps.

Willa-Mae's mailbox was one of the old letterboxes that probably came with the house, and it made it that much easier when I cast the screen. To everyone else, I looked like a mail carrier sticking Willa-Mae's mail into the box.

Keeping my hand steady, I did my best to work the key into the lock. It gave a final click and I creaked the door open, hoping no unexpected guests were here.

"Hello? Is anyone here?" I whispered loudly, checking for human and animals alike. I'd seen one of Willa-Mae's cats in the window before and had my own experience with pesky animals not wanting to leave.

There were still a few bowls filled with cat food and water shoved up under a nearby antique end table. But as far as I could tell, the cats were gone and I was alone.

If I were a crabby woman's cell phone, where would I be? The pantry door was half open and I considered it. No. That would seem like someone intentionally placed it there. It needed to be somewhere she'd actually leave it.

I finally landed on stuffing the phone deep between two of the couch cushions, figuring it made the most sense. I was out of the house just as quickly and quietly as I'd come, my heartbeat easing back up once I stepped foot back in the cemetery.

The space around me was strewn with weeds. I sat back on my heels, groaning as I clutched my back. One thing I was surely going to miss was my complimentary Monday massages at the MGM Grand's spa. Two hours of pulling weeds and I was in need of a back rub and a shoulder massage.

I needed to call a lawn care company to mow the whole place until I could save up and buy my own lawn mower. It was a necessary expense, but I hated paying someone to do something I could very well do myself. Call it the stubborn witch in me.

I started to get the feeling I was being watched, and sure enough as I looked over my shoulder I saw Geena strolling up the yard.

"Hello. Hard at work?" she said, smiling down at me.

I shielded my eyes. "Something like that. These darn things have completely taken over everything in the flower beds. Such as shame—I can tell there were some beautiful roses here."

"Oh, Hazel loved the rosebushes. They put out lilac blooms the most—her favorite color."

"Your friend who lived here?"

She nodded. "She was everyone's friend. A good woman."

I pushed myself up to my feet and dusted off my old jeans. "She was lucky to have so many people in her life. Oh! That reminds me... I washed up that casserole dish for you. It was so delicious, by the way. I ate on it for a couple days until there wasn't a scrap left. Any chance you'd mind giving me the recipe?"

Geena grinned. "I don't know about handing over my Nana's secret green bean casserole recipe. She might just turn over in her grave."

I leaned in, pretending to whisper. "What she don't know won't hurt her."

"Well, in that case..."

We both laughed and talked gardening for a few minutes, Geena telling me about her uninspiring geraniums.

"And my azalea bushes. Ugh, they're so droopy this year. Usually I can get some good magenta and coral blooms from them. I planted them twenty some-odd years ago and never had a problem with them."

"I do love a good azalea bush," I replied, sympathizing.

"You know who was always worrying over the state of

everyone's yards, though?" Her gaze swept the trees beside the cemetery.

"I have a feeling I know. She seemed like the type of person who would reign high and mighty on an HOA."

"Ain't it the truth? I don't like to speak ill of the deceased, but Willa-Mae sure did love her an argument. If no one wanted to contribute, she'd just start mining for trouble until she struck gold. She had enough room in her mouth for ten more rows of teeth, that one."

Nodding, I folded my arms across my chest. The more I heard about Willa-Mae Hurst, the more I found it easier to imagine someone wanting her gone. It was terrible but true. And with the Sheriff now questioning my alibi—according to the way he called me yesterday and 'checked' to see if I had anything else to share with him about the matter—I was itching for them to hurry up and find the real murderer.

"Why was she like that? So bitter and resentful, I mean. She actually told me my house was cursed. Can you believe it?"

This time Geena was the one looking concerned. "She told you that? Heavens to Betsy... Her and Hazel didn't get along. Even before Willa-Mae moved into the house.

I raised a brow. "You mean she hasn't always lived in her house?"

"No ma'am. She moved in early last year. It's a pretty unique story, actually. Her house was up for auction at the monthly town hall meeting. There were plenty of people interested in the property from what I heard. Anyway, someone at the meeting got the idea in their head that they could use the house in a more beneficial way to the town. Nella is just a little place compared to other cities around us, and the schools needed some better funding.

They decided to take the house off of public auction and offer it as the grand prize for a charity to benefit the school system. A bingo game, rather. The tickets were ten dollars a

Bingo sheet and they made a killing. The whole town showed up—who doesn't want a free house, after all?"

My jaw dropped. "Wait a minute. You're telling me she won the house in a *bingo game?* And I thought I'd seen it all…"

Geena just laughed. "Nothing but the truth!"

A thought occurred to me, spurred by the new information. "Something like that's bound to cause some friction among people. Don't you think?"

She seemed to be following my train of thought. "I do, indeed. It's something I've been wondering about myself."

Biting my lip, I wondered if it was necessary to come right out and say it or not. After all, Geena was the one who had come over to chat. She must not think so poorly of me if that were the case.

"I didn't do it. I know people are whispering about me," I said, sighing. "The Sheriff isn't much better. He seems to think I'm holding back from him."

"Don't fret on it, darlin'. Everyone will have their opinion one way or the other. And once the real culprit is found you'll be off the hook with Harry—er, Sheriff Paine. And I certainly don't think you did it, Birdie." Geena tapped her finger to her temple with a sly grin. "I've got an eye for sussing people out."

"Oh?" Was Geena a witch and I just didn't know it?

"I'm observant when others aren't. I suppose it's part of being a nurse, retired or not. I'm a good judge of character, and I can tell the kind of person you are."

A slight twitch in my stomach had me wringing my gloved hands. "And what kind of person is that?"

She took a few steps back, pretending to analyze me. "Kind but guarded. You enjoy being around people, but you aren't an easy nut to crack. Independent—probably pretty stubborn about it, too. You like to stay busy, so you're someone who has a lot on their mind. Maybe even a few things you don't want people knowing. And you like fashion.

Your earrings are from Tiffany's—I know because Francine's husband Harry bought her the same pair last year and we all ooh'ed and aah'ed over them. Am I close?"

I tilted my head, my mind racing. "Very. How do you…?"

"It's nothing. Like I said, I'm observant. That's actually why I came over here. You look like you could use some girl talk to brighten your week up. Why don't you come on over to Bubba-Rays around lunch time tomorrow around noon and meet the rest of the girls? They'd love to get to know you."

It was a big risk, admittedly. Especially seeing how observant Geena was. I didn't want to disappoint the only one who'd extended an olive branch to me.

"Well, I don't think I have any plans…"

Geena's eyes lit up. "Perfect! Then we'll see you then. I've got to get back to my groceries at home. Hopefully the ice cream hasn't melted!"

I thanked her for stopping by and waved as she walked back toward her house. Looking down at the piles of weeds I still needed to bag up, I frowned.

Maybe making new friends wouldn't be so bad. But then again, I wasn't sure what I would do if one of them found out the truth about me being a witch.

Did I want to take that chance?

9

1901

"Grifter. Won't you be a dear and bring me that sledgehammer?"

Sweat was pouring down every inch of me, and I wiped off my clammy palms, grabbing my phone from the counter.

"Hello? Yes, this is she. Oh, wonderful! Yes, I'd like to go ahead and get that started," I said, answering the phone. Wires were hanging out all around the lower level of the house, in need of newly insulated wiring, thanks to my little bit of know-how. But I still had a lot to learn, and I had to bite the bullet and call an electrician to come out after all.

Once I set up the appointment for the following afternoon, I leaned against the refrigerator. The light humming coming from it left me in a daze as I tried to recall everything that was next on my list hanging up behind my back.

"The electric work will be taken care of tomorrow… I think. I just need to finish tearing out this insulation. Shouldn't be. Too. Hard."

Grifter trotted into the kitchen, looking as indifferent as ever. He sniffed at the leftover sandwich that was half-wrapped. I eyed him, my eyes narrowing.

"Don't you even think about it."

I grabbed the sandwich from small dining room table I'd just snagged this morning from the flea market and stuck it in the refrigerator, shaking my head. "You know, you're an odd dog. You sniff the scent right out of everything, but you never want to take a bite. You're like my paranoid grandmother—she never wanted to eat anything others prepared for her. It used to drive me crazy."

It was true. Grandmother usually cooked and baked everything in our house. Her youngest daughters—my twin aunts, Vivienne and Lilian—could hardly cook because of it. I made sure I taught myself as a child because I wasn't about to become a woman with no skills.

Such a difference from when I first lived here to now. My stars, there was an even bigger difference between the glamor of Las Vegas and Nella in 1901. If I'd known how my life would turn out back then, I could have saved myself years of grief over leaving in the first place.

Without even meaning to, I sat down at the little table and unwrapped the bandana from my head. It still felt like walking into a dream sometimes, walking around Nella. When I was in line at the grocery market I'd let my memories get the best of me and nearly dropped my eggs as I put them on the conveyor belt, as I stared out the front of the store. Across the street was where the first schoolhouse was built.

Of course it was used for some kind of warehouse now, but I remembered wishing day after day that Grandmother would let me attend school with some of the other young girls I saw walking around town. I let my mind wander some more, thinking about how mad I'd been when she last told me no…

. . .

"We're not to go mixing with the rest of the town," she said in her stern voice, ending the conversation just as abruptly as I brought it up.

"But... Grandmother! I should go to learn, just like—"

She cut her eyes at me and pursed her lips as we fixed the silky black tablecloth across our seance table. "Silly wishes. There's nothing some so-called educated teacher can teach you that you can't learn here. Besides. We need you here for the business."

I grit my teeth. Some kind of business—my aunties charming the pants off of any passersby, convincing them to reach out to their dearly departed through our spiritual services.

Vivienne waltzed into the meeting room, her long black hair already rolled and pinned under just as her and Lilian preferred. She glared at me and swiped her gloved finger over one of the gaslit wall sconces on the wall.

"Mother, we can't have our guests sitting in these conditions. The room is practically a pigsty."

In my head, I counted until Grandmother turned and looked me over disapprovingly.

"She's right, Birdie. We'll need the good furniture wax—the one I concocted, of course. Please tend to these," she said, waving her hand around the room.

I knew better than to argue with my elders, most especially Grandmother, so I kept my lips pressed together and went to the curio cabinet where she kept all of her potions and tinctures.

Lilian came up behind me, shaking my shoulder as I shut the door to the cabinet, nearly scaring the soul right out of me. "Good morning, Bird-Legs. Does Grandmother already have you cleaning up?" Her smirk reminded me of a cat keeping close watch on a mouse.

"Yes," I simply replied, stepping around her. "We have guests on their way."

She stood in front of one of the mirrors in our tiny parlor, patting her white blonde hair. "Hm. I better get into position, then."

Both she and Vivienne took their seats at the round meeting table, exchanging the look that kept me on my guard. They may have been grown women and a full ten years older than me, but they reminded me more of the girls my age who gossiped in the park whenever I was near. Spiteful. Ugly in a way that only the devil could see. And it didn't matter that I was supposed to be grown enough to handle myself—they treated me as a small child as often as they could.

I took to cleaning the tabletop, doing my best to ignore the way the twins held a whole conversation about me as if I wasn't there. My cheeks burned hot as Vivienne shouted at me to hurry up.

But this was how it was every day. Grandmother wasn't so much cruel to me, as very strict about how I should act. The business was nothing more than conning innocent people out of their hard-earned wages by telling them they could communicate with the dead on their behalf.

Not that it wasn't true, but what they did was nothing of the sort—it would 'eat away at our energy' too much as Grandmother explained it. Instead, they used tricks and misdirection to make our guests believe in my Aunties' powers. In Nella, Vivienne and Lilian Devaine were known as the Tele-Twins. Vivienne had the power of telepathy, while Lilian had the power of telekinesis.

It was my job to have all of their little tricks and everything set up prior to the guests coming by. I was also in charge of helping Grandmother developing the photos and manipulating them to appear as though there were spirits in the photo as well. I finished up, wishing for the guest to hurry up and arrive. At the very least I could be out of the dark and deceiving room and free from the three of them. For now…

10

THE GALS

"And you're sure you don't need me here while you're working?"

Franklin, the lovely older gentleman who was heading up the two-man electrical crew, nodded without looking my way. He was bent over an exposed socket.

"Yes, ma'am. You don't have to sit here and watch us—you'd be better off watching paint dry. Don't worry—I'm an honest man. And my son is too. Plus, I'd still whoop him if he tried pulling something. I don't care if he's a grown man, ain't that right, boy?"

His son, who was easily in his mid-thirties just shook his head. I could see the corner of his mouth turning up though. "Sure, Pops. You've been saying that for as long as I can remember."

"It's as true now as it was when you were running around in nothin' but a diaper, too." Franklin turned to me. "We'll keep an eye on the place. And feel free to lock up behind yourself if it makes you feel any better."

"That's quite all right. I trust you, gentlemen. I suppose I'll be on my way then..."

Truthfully, it wasn't that I was hesitant about leaving the

house to a couple of strangers working on a potentially dangerous aspect of the renovation.

You're stalling. You know darn well what you're wringing your hands over.

I glanced at my watch as I bid them goodbye, sighing to myself. Geena had extended the invitation to me to have lunch with her and her friends, and I still wasn't one-hundred percent sure I was ready for that just yet.

Not to mention the fact that Sheriff Paine alluded to believing me to be a main suspect in Willa-Mae's death. His words at the sheriff's department echoed in my head as I drove. There was an implicit meaning behind them. If they were so worried about the wrong person, then what was happening with the actual killer? It was hard to sleep a wink at night, knowing that they could be out there, watching.

The drive downtown went by much quicker than usual, and before I knew it I was pulling up alongside of the main stretches of businesses. A few doors down was the end of the block where a '50s style diner was flashing it's neon light in the window that read 'Bubba Ray's Hot Lunch Now!'

Bubba Ray was certainly doing well. Though the outside of the diner was simple and reminded me of another time in history, the inside was spacious, clean and a beautiful mix of the turn of the century modern, and the actual modern. Impressive.

Each person wearing a 'Bubba Ray's' apron was wearing a white hat to match the style. All I could think about was my favorite malt back when I lived in Massachusetts in the early '50s. Right after I'd divorced that lowlife, Richard.

I was of half a mind to order a strawberry malt just to be spiteful in his memory.

"Birdie!" Geena's voice rang out like a bell, higher than I remembered. But when I turned around I realized that it wasn't Geena calling me over. Another woman I'd seen in the cul de sac was standing at the table in the farthest corner, waving at me with a huge smile to match her wide eyes.

I hesitated. The woman was sitting between two other women who were also not Geena. Even though I knew they were the other women I was meeting here, I tried to pretend that maybe I was wrong, and Geena said another time to meet up.

"For crying in a bucket, Frannie, stop waving your arm around like that. You're shaking the whole table," I overheard the shorter woman scowl at her.

Frannie didn't pay her any mind and beckoned me anyway. "Come on over! We saved you a seat!"

I nervously glanced back toward the door, secretly hoping that Geena would be coming in at that exact moment, all I saw was the sign blinking in the window.

Well. Nothing to it but to grin and bear it. Keeping my head held high, I walked over to them, preparing to dazzle them with the best smile I could muster.

"Are you all right? You're not one of those women all doped up on pain pills and botox, are you?" the shorter woman said, leaning back in her chair with a speculative look on her face.

I blinked. "I'm not... what?"

"Oh, don't mind TJ. She's not spayed," said the woman who was chuckling on the other side of Frannie. TJ flipped her off, still leaning back in her chair.

"I'm Cinda Beaumont," the other woman said, sticking her hand out with a grin. "This is Frannie, Francine, that is. And that one there is TJ. My cousin."

Hm. My sympathies to Cinda then.

I smiled back at her, realizing I may have been a tad too overly friendly walking over. "It's nice to meet you all. I'm Birdie Devaine."

Frannie squealed as she sat down, pointing to one of the

two available chairs. "Have a seat! Geena should be here before too long."

I nodded and did just that, settling my purse on the back of the chair. The four of us all stared at each other, wearing different apprehensive looks on our faces.

Cinda at least had the decency to order us a pitcher of sangria. I took a good look around the place, still finding little surprises here and there. What kind of '50s style diner served sangria?

"Bubba's a good friend of mine. I went to high school with him—we were sweethearts actually, before he joined the service," Cinda said, thanking the waitress as she set the glass pitcher full of red fruit and drink in the middle of our table. "And we'll need a little while to decide lunch, Brittany, hun. Geena's on her way now."

Brittany swung her hair off her shoulder and smiled. "Take your time, ladies."

Cinda turned her attention back to me. "He doesn't bust this out for just anyone." With a wink she poured a glass and handed it to me. "It's good enough to whet your whistle after a long days' work."

I took a long sip, satisfied with the mixture of tart wine and sweet bits of strawberry. "My, that is good."

"Told ya! Bubba knows his stuff."

Frannie darn near finished her glass and sat back, her wide eyes watching me. "So Birdie, what brings you to Nella? Geena didn't really fill in all the details just yet."

Oh boy. There was nothing I hated more than talking about myself. Actually scratch that—my Aunties. I hated them worse than even the most mundane ice breaking conversations.

I was fully well aware that TJ was eyeing me rather suspiciously. I didn't know what I did to draw her ire, but it was already clear to me that we weren't getting off on the best foot.

Clearing my throat carefully, I slid my glass away and smiled. "I was looking for a nice place to settle down."

TJ snorted. "And of all the places you could choose from, you picked Nella? Heck... you picked Mississippi?"

Both Cinda and Frannie groaned at TJ's outburst.

So. This was what I was dealing with. I've known my share of bullies in my life, and I wasn't about to cater to this one, either. "I grew up in Mississippi, so yes. And Nella is, despite its size, a perfect place to settle down for some peace and quiet."

"I think it's a great choice, too. Harry and I have lived here our whole lives. We raised our family here. You won't find me complaining!" Frannie said with the kind of joy in her voice that I usually found forced. But coming from her, it was genuine.

"I've lived here my whole life too, woman. Doesn't mean nothin'," TJ muttered, pursing her lips at me before tossing the straw out of her glass and chugging a big gulp down.

"My kids spread out as soon as they were able to—but me and Danny are still here. I must like this place if I bought a firehouse here," Cinda said as-a-matter-of-factly.

I raised a brow. "A firehouse?"

"Yep. The old firehouse on Porter Avenue. I bought it five years ago and turned it into The Macaroon Boutique."

"Cinda is a world-class pastry chef!" Frannie announced. "That sweet fella—what was his name again, Cinda?"

"Oh, here we go again," TJ groaned and dropped her head into her hand.

"Adrien Zumbo. Real nice guy—kind of goofy. He's a top pastry chef in Australia. TJ liked him somethin' fierce, didn't you?" she laughed, nudging her cousin's arm.

TJ slapped her hand away, glaring. "I swear you were put on this earth to annoy the mess out of me. I knew it the moment you were born."

Cinda simply rolled her eyes, her and Frannie both

chuckling together. "You knew all that at the ripe ol' age of three, did you? Don't be embarrassed, Tully. We all know you still have that old napkin with his signature stashed away somewhere in your house."

"Ladies. Now, now. I'm gone for barely a day and this is what happens? Look at them, Birdie. Grown and still in need of a babysitter."

Geena stood behind me, sneaking up on us all. She placed a hand on my shoulder and squeezed. "I'm glad you took me up on my offer. I hope these three haven't scared you off already."

I shook my head. "I don't scare easily."

"Anyway, Birdie! Cinda's got the best beignets and macarons this side of the Mississippi— even that fancy chef thought so," Frannie continued on. "Absolutely to die for!"

From what I gathered, Frannie probably said that about just about anything she liked.

"You never really told us anything about you," TJ observed, taking another swig from her glass.

"What's there to know?" I replied, my voice a little on the edge.

She shrugged as Geena sat down next to me. "Well for starters, we can talk about that fake accent of yours."

"Tullulah-Jean!" Geena gasped. "What on God's green pastures are you thinking? Sorry about her, Birdie. She's clearly off her meds."

TJ didn't back down though. The glint in her eye made me wonder if she didn't enjoy putting people in their place. Pfft. Who was I kidding? Of course she did.

"Hm. Well, considering that it's as real as I am standing in front of you, there isn't much to talk about in that respect." Ooh, I wanted so badly to turn that umbrella by her foot into a snake—or at least make her think it was.

"Why do you sound like you're rehearsing for the local rendition of Gone with the Wind, then?" she countered.

All I could do was smile—kill 'em with kindness was one of the first rules of being a lady in the south of course. "Scarlett O'Hara was a mighty fine lady. I'll take that as a bonafide compliment, Miss Tullulah-Jean."

Oh, she didn't like that. Not one bit. She seethed as Geena cleared her throat. "I must agree with Birdie. I do love that movie. Rhett Butler? My mama had quite a thing for him. 'Frankly my dear, I don't give a damn,' was like her motto when I was a kid."

I chuckled. "Your mama sounds like a smart lady."

"She was, bless her. And sweet as pecan pie. Never knew a stranger."

Cinda nodded, throwing an arm around Geena. "Miss Claire was like our second mother growing up. Back before me, TJ, and Geena ended up on Witch Hazel Lane, we lived a few blocks away from one another. Miss Claire would have us all come have supper every Sunday night after church. My parents didn't mind, they were too busy with their own things to worry about me. And TJ—well, Uncle Jerome and Aunt Patti couldn't keep her inside to save their tails."

"Oh, so you've known each other for your whole lives?" I said with surprise in my voice. I'd never known anyone for that long, much less spent that much time with them.

"That's how it is for most of us here. Small town, you know. We don't get out much," TJ said slowly, as if she were speaking to a child.

I chose to ignore her. Sometimes you had to take the higher ground.

"Frannie moved here from Texas back in '86. She was nearly ready to pop when her and Harry moved in. Joanna was born what, four days later?" Cinda asked, squinting her eyes at Frannie.

"Oh yes. Four days on the nose. She's my only girl," Frannie said, turning to me. "Jack, Jonathan, and James are my boys. Triplets."

"Oh my stars..." I said softly. "That is... a lot of testosterone in one household. I bet your husband ate it up."

Everyone at the table laughed at the comment.

"Those boys nearly drove him to drinking," Frannie said just as breezy as could be. "I love them to bits of course. They just needed kept in line. It's one of the reasons he joined the force."

"The force?" I asked.

"He's the Deputy Sheriff. You met him the other day, I believe," she said.

Well. There goes the neighborhood. "Right. Yes, yes I did. I suspect that he is very good at his job."

She grinned proudly, slipping a chain that was dangling past her collar out for me to see. "He's a good man, through and through. He saved up and bought me this for our fiftieth anniversary last year. Isn't it beautiful?"

The necklace was modest compared to many of the ones I'd worn for my shows—all loaners of course. But I smiled. It was simple but very obviously given with love. "Yes, ma'am. It matches your eyes."

Blush colored her cheeks. "Thank you, Birdie. Hazel thought so too."

The table's energy was sucked away immediately. Even TJ's sourpuss expression faded.

"Hazel Hampton. It was her home, correct?" I asked gently.

"Used to be. Before her family sold it to the county. It was meant to be a historical landmark. Registered and everything. Hazel wanted to wash her hands clean of that old place," TJ said, her voice quiet and thoughtful. It was a sharp contrast to the rest of her words.

I couldn't pretend to know what she meant, but I had a feeling it was something deeper.

"Speaking of the Hampton House..." Geena was the first person to speak up again. "How's the renovating going?"

Now this was something I could go on about. Innocent enough without giving too much up. "Well, as far as I know. I've never renovated a house before, so each day it's like finding a new surprise and going on a new journey. By journey I mean traveling through the hallway or from the kitchen to the veranda mind you, but it's keeping me busy."

"I hope you don't mind me asking, but why did you pick that house in particular?" Frannie said. She was fishing for more background info on me, if I had to bet.

"I saw it and found where it was—the whole Queen Anne style of it is something I really admire. It's my favorite style of architecture."

"Let's get down to the nuts and bolts of it. What happened to Willa-Mae?" TJ caught me so off guard that it was like a punch to the gut. They had no way of knowing anything of course, but I certainly wasn't expecting the complete detour of the conversation.

"What... happened? I haven't a clue. She was found in the middle of the night off the side of the road between our properties. Right by the cemetery."

TJ gestured for me to continue and since the other three were clearly intent on hearing it, I sighed and told them exactly what I told Sheriff Paine.

"I didn't know her really, but it's tragic, truly," I finished it off. "Was she... a friend of yours?"

"Ha! That old cuckoo bird? She's no more a friend to us than the man in the moon," Cinda spoke up this time, slapping her thigh. "Don't look so shocked, hun. Willa-Mae Hurst wasn't a pleasant kind of woman."

Well, at least someone had said it and it wasn't me.

"Either way. No one deserves that," Frannie said, her tone somber. "Harry told me she was likely choked to death."

They all went on to explain different incidents with Willa-Mae that only further proved Cinda's point. I listened in, not surprised to hear it. I knew she'd been trouble.

"The question is though, who did it? We know practically everyone in town! I can't think of a single soul who would do something so wretched," Frannie said in a scandalized whisper.

"I think we all know a few scumbags who aren't worth the key to lock them up," TJ said, following it up with a humorless laugh.

"They're just bad apples, Tully. Just because they have the brains of fleas doesn't mean they're going around choking poor old ladies out," Cinda said, rolling her eyes.

"You're calling Gus Barnaby a bad apple? That's putting it a little too nicely, if you ask me," TJ replied.

"Shh, shh," Frannie said, nodding to something behind me. All of us none too subtly turned to see what she was looking at.

A tall man with a gut like Grandmother's mint jelly shoved open the front door causing the bell to ring harshly above him. His eyes were far too small for the roundness of his face, and his arms in proportion to the rest of his bulky figure reminded me somewhat of a gorilla in the jungle.

"This is Gus, I take it?" I nudged Geena as quiet as possible.

She nodded but didn't say a word.

TJ, on the other hand, didn't seem to mind at all if she was overheard. "That's right. Not worth the key to lock him up. Look at him strolling in here acting like he owns the place. He does that at Cinda's place, too. Smug sonuva--"

"Shh!" Geena hushed her louder.

I took another good look at the man, and I could feel the heavy energy rolling off of him in waves. His aura was weak, but it was tinged here and there with a deep red. So he had anger issues.

Interesting.

11
BUBBA-RAYS

The brisket sandwich sat half-eaten on my plate as I listened to Geena tell me about her years as a Med-Surge nurse at the local hospital. I'd seen plenty of things in my lifetime, I was practically a Jill of all trades at this point, but I'd never been as passionate about any of them quite the way Geena was about being a nurse.

"Of course, I still renew my license every year. I'll never *not* be a nurse," she explained, polishing off her pulled pork.

"She calls it taking a siesta," TJ said, rolling her eyes. It seemed to me that this was TJ's favorite pastime.

But Geena just shrugged. "Just because I'm retired, doesn't mean I'm useless."

"Hun, no one would ever say that about you—not in a million years," Cinda said.

There was something comforting in listening to the four of them, even though I was mostly a spectator. It was much nicer than I originally thought it would be. But a pang of loneliness still ached in my chest. If Corinne were here she'd have some stories to tell, too. Even as young as she was, she'd worked with all sorts of celebrities before, all of whom gave her the inside scoop about anything and everything. You'd be surprised at what kind of hijinks go on behind the scenes of the so-called beautiful people's lives.

A far cry from Vegas, Bubba Ray's diner was playing host to the lunch hour crew now, the line to be seated went halfway out the door. Apparently the place was a hot commodity around here.

As more and more people found empty seats, I felt included in the conversation the ladies were having and tried to listen to them only.

I was finding that almost impossible. It wasn't as though I had super hearing (though I'd met some witches who truly did), it was just hard not to overhear some of the people sitting around us in the diner, even over the din of everyone else's voices.

One lady was fussing at her husband for choosing to take her here, instead of the Olive Garden, Nella's only slightly fine dining establishment. Another few men were busy going over some football team's stats.

I forgot just how much people in the south love their college football.

And then I heard it. Just a hushed conversation nearby at another table.

"I think we should find out just who we're dealing with here. What if this is just some fancy government ploy to keep us better controlled? Witches. Ha. They could've at least been a little cleverer than all that."

As soon as they devolved into talking about a registration list I checked out of the conversation completely.

Cinda and Frannie were busy talking about Cinda needing a new haircut, and TJ was going back and forth between staring at this Gus fellow and finishing her lunch.

Whatever the case was, TJ clearly wasn't a fan of his. With that kind of energy and the smug look on his face, I was starting to see why.

"That man is fixin' to get his tires slashed," TJ said,

making a face at someone behind Geena and me. I snuck a peek only to realize that it was this Gus guy. He was unabashedly glaring at us, at TJ in particular.

"I don't know how you could ever stand to be around him, Geena." TJ said, shaking her head.

"It wasn't as if I had much choice," Geena said, waiting until she was finished with her food before continuing on. "Darren did all the new-hires. And Gus doesn't work on the med-surge floor. He was usually down at the morgue."

"Who is this Gus guy?" I asked, following along with interest. Anyone who earned the ire of Geena and her friends was probably the kind of person I wanted to avoid at all costs.

"He's a leech. He's always looking for handouts and has never worked a hard day in his life, for starters," Cinda answered. She leaned forward with her chin in her hand. "Geena had to deal with him and his shenanigans for five years."

"Leech, ha. Leeches are too good for him. He's like the dirt and gravel that gets stuck between the tread in your tires. Except at least that stuff gets ran over. I pray, but it never seems to happen to him.

"Tully! That's ridiculous. You can't say things like that," Frannie gasped, half-whispering.

"Well," TJ replied, very obviously doing her best not to look at him anymore. "It's not like I'm lyin'."

"To put it mildly, Birdie, that man is nothing but trouble. He doesn't mind screwing someone over if he gets what he wants out of the deal. I worked with a lovely lady named Miranda—she was an orderly. She was fired over something that was ultimately Gus's fault, and instead of being a man and owning up to his mistake, he spun a tale instead, telling the resident doctor on the floor that he'd caught her doing his mistake, as well as throwing in some other little fibs to help cover his rear-end."

If the man hadn't been sitting twenty feet behind me, I would've let out a whistle. "He sounds like a real piece of work."

She nodded and folded her arms across her chest. "He's something, all right."

Without being too obvious, I positioned myself in a way so that I could look at him again. Much to everyone's dismay, Gus still had his beady little eyes trained on us. It wouldn't have been quite so unnerving if he had the decency to look away when he saw us looking right back at him. But I had a feeling that didn't bother him like it should.

Gus barked a laugh as he clapped one of his buddies on the shoulder, finally looking away. "I told you brother. They never pay attention to that stuff. The board's so worried about bleeding money that they haven't even upgraded the system in twenty years. I'm talking Windows 98."

Geena's fork scraped across the plate suddenly, and she paused. I may not have been a telepath like Lilian, but I could tell when someone was listening in and sifting through someone else's conversation.

I figured what the heck, and did my best to block out all the other noise so I could hear what Gus was saying as he turned so that we could no longer see his face.

There were bits and pieces I could just make out were enough to make anyone do a double take. "When you have an in like that... it's all so easy... make a ton... don't even have to hack it, you just... how I paid for my pontoon boat."

Geena, who was intently focused on her plate, held on to her fork so tightly that I was worried for the fork. Her face was a deep scarlet.

"You okay?" I whispered to her, still looking back at that loudmouth. He reminded me of those men walking along the strip at night with women on their arms. The ugly men who practically sold their souls to make a buck—their attitude and egos suffered terribly. I'd seen some before—heck,

I even married one. Too little too late with Richard, though.

She pursed her lips and straightened her composure. "I don't understand how people can be so glib about ruining someone else's life."

"What do you mean?"

Geena drew in a deep breath. "Changing medical records —it can be disastrous for the patient, not to mention leave the hospital liable."

Then it hit me. I knew he didn't seem like a charmer but changing someone's medical history doing goddess-knows what to it…that was truly the scariest bit. Not to mention everything he was saying to his friends over there. He practically had them eating out of the palm of his hand.

Gus was busy picking something out of his teeth with a toothpick, his eyes shifting between our table and his buddies. "The thing is fellas, you learn to seize an opportunity no matter what. Me and my family didn't have everything handed to us on a silver platter like some folks around here do," he said loud enough for nearly everyone in the diner to hear.

If I didn't know any better, I would think he craves the attention. Just like those housewives with the TV show following them around all day…

"If he doesn't pipe down…" TJ muttered, pouring herself another glass of sangria. "he's going to see my bag upside his head."

"I never got so much as a handshake from my old man, but you have those old broads living on their husband's money on that fancy street." There was a general murmur of consensus to this, and Gus waved them all off. "Now fellas, you don't want to upset the grannies."

The man sitting directly across from Gus laughed. "Or else they won't knit you a sweater for Christmas."

"Or bake you your favorite cookies."

"Don't expect that twenty in your birthday card this year."

Oh, they think they're clever.

By now everyone at our table had dropped the conversation and were all listening intently to Gus and his charming friends.

Forks and knives scraped across plates everywhere else but here. Even sweetie pie Frannie had her round eyes narrowed at the good 'ol boys.

"Problem, ladies?" Gus said to us, causing everyone in the diner to look our way. His gaze swept the table as if he were personally challenging each one of us.

"Ignore him... Ignore him," Geena said, turning back to her plate.

"Hasn't your mama ever told you it's rude to stare?" TJ called across the diner to him.

"Hard not to. Not with the Grim Reaper in your corner, just biding his time."

Frannie smacked her manicured hand down on the table. "That's enough out of you, Mr. Barnaby! Or have you forgotten how lenient the sheriff's been with you lately?" she shouted, then turning to us to add, "Harry had to take him in for peeing in the playground last weekend. He was drunker than a skunk and could barely stand up straight. Not to mention having trouble pulling his darn trousers up."

"Bullies are boring," I said, pretending to yawn. "I've never quite understood the point of them, really."

"It's the only quality he has—to be a pain in everyone else's butt. That man is just as crooked as a dog's hind leg. And twice as dirty." TJ said. I nearly spit out my sangria, and carefully dabbed at the corner of my mouth with the napkin, doing my best not to laugh.

"Just out of curiosity, what did he do to you?"

"What do you mean?" she replied, leaning forward in her seat.

I thought it was rather obvious what I meant. "I can see

why everyone has reservations about him—but you seem particularly irritated by him. I was just wondering if there was a reason behind it, is all."

TJ studied me for a moment before shrugging. "He was a menace even when he was boy. His daddy ran out on them and his mama didn't do much better by sticking around. He was always harassing Ruby, wasn't he, Geena? We'd be out and he would be walking home from one of his wrestling tournaments at the high school, heckling Ruby and the rest of us. Ruby's what, six or seven years younger than him? It wasn't right. Nowadays he's just a hateful creature. If I was a churchgoer, I'd pray for him. I'd pray for him to go up to the pearly gates and drop through a trap-door straight into Hell."

No one else at the table batted an eye. "I see. I'll make sure not to go walking in his direction then, I suppose."

As if on cue, Gus raised his voice. "Imagine living in some hoity-toity neighborhood and thinkin' you're better than everyone else. High-falutin' trophy wives only making it off their husband's money. I almost feel sorry for the husbands."

I ground my teeth together, understanding just how Geena and her friends really felt about him.

Geena rose quietly from her seat. "I think I speak for everyone in this establishment when I say the only thing everyone wants to hear is the sound of that woodfire grill going in the back. Whatever you're aiming to do, Mr. Barnaby, it won't work. I suggest enjoying your food and company like the rest of us."

Gus's expression changed from smug to elated. You could just tell that he was happy to get a rise out of her. "And I suggest you mind your own dang business, Geena. Don't think you've got the brass ones to tell me what to do."

This time TJ stood up with Geena. "Boy, you're about as sharp as a bowl full of mashed potatoes—sit down and shut up before Francine has to call her husband to come and talk some sense into your small brain. At least maybe this time you won't have to walk back to the car with your pants around your ankles."

Gus shook his head, not exactly unfazed but more like not quick enough on his feet to make a sound come-back. "I'd be more worried about finding yourselves keeled over in the cemetery like that old hag."

The whole diner seemed to go quiet.

"All right. That's enough of that, big boy. Time to get packin'," a deep voice bellowed from the kitchen doorway. The man easily stood six and a half feet tall, his arms bulging through his t-shirt sleeves they were so muscular. If I had to hazard a guess, he was retired military—mid to late fifties. Something about the way his dark eyes regarded Gus reminded me of something… but I couldn't quite put my finger on it.

Gus sputtered, clearly not counting on getting kicked out of the diner. "Bubba! I ain't do nothing! I'm a paying customer—you can't just boot me out of here like that!"

"Boy," Bubba-Ray said, his voice rumbling. "You see that sign on the window there? That's my name—it's by the grace I give you that you're eating that fine sandwich in front of you. When it comes to my diner, I can do what I please."

Gus and his friends looked utterly put-out. One of them hesitated as he reached to the last of his French-fries. He looked around and scooped up some from his plate, others around them snickering.

Gus pushed away from the table hard enough to make the whole thing rattle, still muttering something or other to himself. He knew he'd been beat.

The rest of the diner clapped as Bubba-Ray pointed his finger toward the door. "That's right—take your food and don't let the door hit ya where the good Lord split ya."

"Thank you, Bubba," Geena sighed as Gus and his goonies shuffled out the door.

He nodded, still watching the three of them until they

were out of sight. "I should start posting a bouncer outside of this place during lunch hour. I'm tired of letting in just any old riffraff."

Geena's cheeks flushed but she smile graciously and thanked him again before he headed back into the kitchen.

Cinda pulled out her purse and rummaged around until she found her lipstick. "If I didn't know any better, I'd say someone has a little crush on the handsome chef."

"Then you mustn't know any better," Geena simply said.

Both Cinda and Frannie stood up, while TJ reluctantly contributed a few dollars to the middle of the table, leaving me and Geena to it. "Keep telling yourself that, darlin'." Cinda turned to me and winked. "It was nice meeting you, Birdie. You'll have to come down and see me at the Macaroon Boutique. I give out free samples for new customers."

"We'll see you around, Birdie," Frannie said, smiling and leaning down to give me a tight squeeze.

"Yeah, yeah. I need to get going. Cinda, you got time to drop me off at Doctor Bailey's office?"

"I might could. Depends on whether you're ready to let Frannie finally get her hands on that mop top or not," Cinda said on the sly, throwing one last wink at me and Geena as she and TJ walked out behind Frannie still arguing as they passed by the diner's front window.

Geena watched them go with a wistful smile on her face. "Those three, I swear."

"They're lovely, honestly," I said, genuinely meaning it. Well, TJ wasn't exactly lovely, but I could see where she might be a good friend if you stayed around long enough to crack her shell.

"I think so. I'm sorry about Gus, though. He wasn't supposed to be part of our lunch."

I waved her off and slipped out a few dollars of my own to add to the tip. "A man like that has no effect on me whatsoever. Don't worry on it. And Geena?"

She raised her brow. "Yes?"

"Thank you for inviting me out. I'll be honest—I wasn't sure whether I wanted to come. I'm… not the best at making friends." It felt silly to say it, but I was relieved to see the look in her eyes soften.

"I find that hard to believe. You seem perfectly friendly to me! Unless you have some kind of deep, dark secret hiding under that pretty head."

A lump formed in my throat but I ignored it and instead, smiled. "Secrets? That would require an adventurous life—and I'm afraid that hasn't been the case."

It wasn't the best way to start off a friendship. But the lie would keep me afloat for a little while.

12
RADIO SILENT

If there was one thing I liked about the hardware store, it was the smell of the wood and sawdust inside.

I pulled out my supply list made by Franklin, who was back at my house bright and early to get started on the wiring upstairs. With the inspector coming at the end of the week, I wanted to make sure I had at least that done.

The big cart squeaked as I pushed it down the right aisle, following the hundreds of things loaded up on each side until I found what I needed.

My pants buzzed. The moment the phone rang in my pocket I picked it up, recognizing the ringtone immediately. Corinne was a huge fan of jazz, so I'd picked one that suited her well.

"Darling! How are you?" I sang into the phone, dropping the bronzed light switch plates down into the cart. I didn't realize how much I missed her until her name flashed across my screen.

She chuckled into the phone. "It's been nuts here, but I'm sure you already know that."

I winced. "That bad, huh?"

"They moved me to the soundstage temporarily. Until they find a new headliner, I guess. I've heard whispers about them getting in touch with a few different people. But you know how long those contracts can take."

"Very true."

"Daria Morrigan *may* or *may not* have been on the list of names."

I groaned. Daria Morrigan had been clamoring for her own show since I first landed the gig at the MGM Grand. I appealed to her manager to see if she wanted to look into a collaborative project together, but Daria shot it down. She was no fan of mine.

"And what about Preston? Is he still lingering around?"

"If by lingering around you mean bugging me over your whereabouts, then yes. He still doesn't believe that I don't know where you are."

I didn't dare check my emails. My texts from him had finally started easing up which only meant that he had more formal things to say to me... and that only meant one thing—he was through working as my manager.

Most people in my situation would be gobsmackingly worried over the whole thing. But I was quite the opposite, funny enough. Between worrying over the house renovation, Sheriff Paine being on my tail, and a killer on the loose, the last thing I was thinking about was how everyone back in Vegas was doing with my sudden disappearance.

Truth be told, I felt a little guilty about it.

"That man knows better than to try to find me when I don't want to be found. I made that plain as day to him the last time we spoke over the phone," I explained, pushing the cart down the next aisle.

There was a pause, and then, "Birdie. Are you okay?"

"What do you mean?" Did I really sound so melancholy?

"I don't know. You leave without telling me goodbye, then I have to find out from Preston that you've not only broken your contract, but you've gone radio silent on us. No one knows where you are or when you're coming back. You've been gone for two weeks and I'm only just now getting ahold of you."

Guilt washed over me. She was absolutely right. I've been so concerned about everything going on here that I hadn't even bothered to check in with her. And while I didn't mind leaving everyone else in the dust, Corinne was a different matter.

I bit my lip. "I'm so sorry, darling. I've been wretched, not calling to check in with you. I should've done that straight away. I'm sorry if you've worrying about me—I assure you I'm doing just fine."

Knowing that I could trust her, I gave her a rundown of everything that had happened in the past two weeks' time. Corinne laughed.

"Only you would buy some old house without ever taking a look at it. No wonder Preston was freaked about all the money being gone from your line of credit. And that whole thing with your neighbor… that's pretty intense."

"Tell me about it. I move here to get away from all of that nonsense and here I end up right smack dab in the middle of it. It's like bad luck has been following me lately." Which was something I'd only just now considered. Maybe now would be a good time to put up some protection charms around the house…

"Oops. I better go—I'll try and catch up with you later this week. And Birdie? Please stay safe, okay?" Corinne said, sounding in a hurry.

"Of course. I always am." For the most part.

By the time I made it to the checkout lane, I had a whole pile of light plates to stack on the conveyor belt. I smiled at the man running the register and started loading everything on to it.

He didn't smile back. In fact, he scowled at me fiercely enough that I took a step back.

"Is there a problem, sir?" I asked, genuinely worried. But then it hit me—I knew this man. Well, not knew him, but I'd just seen him before a few days ago at Bubba-Ray's Diner. He was one of that no-good's friends who'd been leering at us. It seemed he remember me, too.

"You're the one who just bought the crazy people's house. If there's a problem it ain't mine." He made some sort of disgusting sound in his throat before ringing up my things.

What was it with these men in this town?

"Birdie!" a familiar voice said, sounding fresh as a daisy. Ruby and the man I assumed was her husband came up in line behind me, with a small basket of things.

"Well, hello. How are you doing today, Ruby?" I said, smiling at her and her husband. "I'm Birdie Devaine, by the way." I extended my hand and he shook it.

"Shawn. Geena was just telling us about you. It's nice to meet you."

"Likewise. What brings you two here on a Saturday morning?" I asked, taking a little peek at what all was inside the basket Ruby was holding. From the looks of it, they were doing some childproofing.

They shared a look and both started laughing, just like how married couples in movies do. With Ruby and Shawn though, I got the feeling it was completely genuine. Out of the corner of my eye I could see Mr. Pleasant Pants' disgusted expression.

"Eva's taken to climbing over the baby gate and up on to the kitchen counter. So it's taking us a little trial and error to figure out how to keep the girl out of things. So far it's been all error," Ruby said, shaking her head. "I thought we had it easy with having a boy and then a girl. Nope."

"No kidding. If Eva would've been born first who knows if Max would've made it onto the scene—not that I don't love my kids of course!" Shawn said, quickly trying to extinguish any negative judgment I may have had on him.

"It's been my experience that the girls are the ones you really have to keep your eye on. Boys can be a handful in the loud, boisterous way, but girls hatch their plans quietly. Without kicking up much fuss." I didn't have a whole lot of experience with children mind you, but I've done my fair share of observing them.

"She's like a little ninja, Birdie, I swear!"

"You done?" Mr. Pleasant Pants said, drawing out his words. "It'll be $36.50."

I did my best to fix a polite smile on my face, despite wanting to wring the rudeness out of him. People like him were the reasons curses existed in the first place. "Thank you," I replied, fiddling with the card reader until it took my payment.

"How is the renovation going, anyway? Mama said you've been working with Franklin? He's wonderful—Shawn uses him and Nathan with the electrical on different work sites."

Shawn nodded, unloading everything from the basket. "He knows his stuff. Franklin is always our first go-to whenever we're doing new construction."

"Oh, you're in construction?" I asked. That would have to be something to file away for another time.

"Yes, ma'am. I took over my father's company last year when he retired. So if you ever need any help with anything, get in touch. We do free estimates for our residential clients." He felt around his pockets until he pulled out his wallet and offered me his business card. "I might even be able to lower the price too, depending on what you need done."

Huh. Well maybe making friends with everyone in the neighborhood really did pay off. "I certainly appreciate it, Shawn."

Once they finished paying, I walked out with them, still chatting with Ruby.

"For cryin' in a bucket! Honey, we forgot to grab a bag of mulch for the front."

Shawn blinked. Ruby smiled innocently up at him, and that was all it took.

He nodded, knowing exactly what she was asking without her even saying a word. "I'll be right back."

Both of us giggled as he turned to walk back into the hardware store. "I haven't seen a man more willing to take one for the team in a long while," I said, still chuckling. "My ex-husband, Cecil was like that, too. Such a sweet man."

"Shawn is definitely that. He works hard and then does anything that I ask of him. I'm a pretty lucky girl," she said, her smile wide. It was sweet seeing just how much she loved him.

"In fact, he's such a good sport that he's happy to let me take some time off to work on my own business. Can you believe that?" Ruby veered to the right, heading in the same direction as my car.

I took a few long strides to keep up with her—she had legs for days apparently. "That's exciting. What kind of business are you working on?"

We stopped outside a red car. The smile on her face faltered. "I'm... not really sure yet."

"Oh." I had no idea what to make of that. If there was one thing I've always prided myself on, it was knowing exactly where the next step was to take. But I knew Ruby was still young. She'd figure things out.

"I know, I know. It sounds silly, right? I know I want to do something different, but I don't know what that different is just yet. Working at the sheriff's department is a secure job, and the benefits are nothing to sneeze at. But it's a little bit..." she trailed off.

"Soul-sucking?" I suggested. I knew a thing or two about a job like that.

"A little bit, yeah. Don't get me wrong, I'm so grateful for even having a job. But sometimes I imagine myself somewhere else doing something that actually makes me happy. And not just sorting through old paperwork and filing evidence into even older boxes." Ruby unlocked the car and put the bag in the trunk with a sad smile on her face.

"There has to be something mildly interesting in that evidence room! You must have the inside scoop on things around town," I said.

"I mean… maybe. I did find out something interesting yesterday while I was doing some record updates. I know I probably shouldn't tell you," she said, dropping her voice low even though there was no one nearby, "I think Willa-Mae might have been an alcoholic. Harry's still waiting on the toxicology reports to come back from upstate, but her clothes reeked of it. It's not much, but it's important to the case anyway."

I took Willa-Mae Hurst as a bitter and nosy type, but something felt off about the idea of her being an alcoholic. Maybe it was because when I did my snooping around with her phone, I hadn't noticed anything that would have suggested so. No empty cans or bottles lying around.

"I wouldn't take her for an alcoholic. Though that is a pretty interesting bit of news."

"Oh, here comes Shawn. It was nice running into you, Birdie. Maybe you can come over for dinner at Mama's house sometime soon. I know she's been dying to get you over there." Ruby yanked open the car door and I waved and started walking toward my car a few spots down.

Maybe it was because Willa-Mae was my neighbor, and she was found on my property… but I felt oddly protective over the case all of the sudden. It hadn't been as much as a necessity to figure out who did it, but the more I thought about it, the more I decided I really wanted to find out.

Only I didn't have the slightest idea how to do that.

13

ALIBI

Franklin's van was still parked way up in the drive when I pulled up to my house. I grabbed my bag of switch plates and screws and headed inside, curious to see how far him and Nathan had gotten on the rewiring upstairs.

Boy was I surprised when I walked into my own house only to see Sheriff Harry Paine standing there, scrolling through his phone.

I stopped dead in my tracks. For Pete's sake, what was he doing here? Much less, in my house when I wasn't?

"Ahem. Sheriff?"

His eyes slid from his phone to me before he tucked it back into a case hanging off of his belt. "Miss Devaine. I didn't see you come in."

I raised a brow. "Well, it is my house." After dealing with the rude man at the hardware store, I was hardly in the mood for another man's bothering.

A small smile broke from the corner of his mouth. He tipped his hat to me. "You're absolutely right. I apologize, I should probably explain why I'm here."

Placing my purse on the end table nearby, I sighed. "I suppose it isn't for a friendly conversation?"

"I think that depends on what you consider friendly conversation. I am here on duty though, if that gives you any idea. It's about the investigation. And uh, I really am sorry if I scared you by being here. The gentleman who's working upstairs let me in after I told him I was looking to speak with you. I hope that's not an issue."

Of course it was. But what's done is done and there was no point in dwelling over it now. "Oh, not at all. I would just advise to wait until I'm home next time. The dog might not like it if I'm not home and someone drops by. And he's not exactly a chihuahua."

Sheriff Paine scratched at his chin, looking around. "You have a dog? Sorry, I didn't realize. Usually I'm real good about knowing when someone has one." He touched his finger to the side of his nose. "Bad allergies to them, you see."

I nodded. "He's an outside dog. I believe. I'm not really sure, actually—he and I are still working on getting acquainted. Anyhow. What can I do for you, Sheriff?"

He glanced around the foyer and into the main parlor. "Is there somewhere we can sit down for a minute?"

"Of course. In the kitchen," I said, not bothering to wait for him to follow. Something didn't settle right in me at the sight of the Sheriff waiting for me inside my house... It wasn't exactly him that bothered me, more like I was unsettled by whatever he might say. What if they figured out that the phone had been moved? Or worse, what if they knew I was the one who moved it?

I was so intent on cutting all possible ties to what happened to Willa-Mae that I had to wonder if maybe I wasn't going about it the wrong way. What if I'd unknowingly left some evidence of my visit there?

Sheriff Paine took the seat by the window and I slid into the seat across from him. I was already sweating more than a sinner in church.

"Have you found out who killed her?" I asked abruptly. There was no point in beating around the bush.

Upstairs, the sound of power tools interrupted the Sheriff when he began to explain. He waited for a moment and continued on. "No, we have not. Rest assured, we're working on it around the clock. These types of things don't usually happen in Nella."

I used to think nothing happened in Nella. I'd been proven wrong every day since I moved back.

"No, I wanted to drop by and let you know that I... I've officially taken you off of the list for questioning." He cleared his throat and leaned forward with his arms on the table. "Not to say that we're not keeping our eyes on things."

I frowned. "Wait. Do you mean you've decided to rule me out as a suspect?" If this was true then I was absolutely relieved... but what convinced them?

Sheriff Paine nodded, but there was some kind of reluctance in his expression. "I've spoken with Gregory Barnaby. He was able to verify your story about working on the title and deed paperwork for the house here. There were timestamps on his digital copies of everything. It lined up with the time of death given by the medical examiner."

Thank goodness for Gregory. I made a mental note to bake him a cake of my own since he was into baking, as a personal thank you for everything.

"Okay, that makes sense," I finally said, still processing it all.

"It makes sense? How so?"

"I thought it was odd that I didn't hear or see anything that night. I... didn't realize it happened while Gregory and I were talking. That... doesn't sit well with me. I feel like we should've known. Maybe we could've done something—scare the person away even."

A fresh, new guilt sunk heavy in my stomach. So it wasn't that I'd been sleeping and soundly unaware of what was happening. It was that I'd been too busy digging into Gregory's cake to worry or notice anything off in the air. I shivered unwillingly.

"Well. We can't blame ourselves for things like these. If you had no part to play in it, then the best you can do is to try and move on. It's something I've learned in the force."

There was a loud bang right overhead and the chandelier swung slightly. He blinked. "I see you're really digging in with the renovation. How is that going, by the way? I haven't been inside this place since the Hamptons threw their last barbecue."

The sudden change of direction left me momentarily dizzy, trying to keep up. "Oh. Yes, it's an ongoing process."

"How long do you think it might take to complete it?"

What was he aiming for? Was the sheriff really that interested in my home renovation project? The knot in my stomach loosened up, but it was most definitely still there.

"Miss Devaine? Are you… all right?"

It took me a second to regain my composure after staring at him blankly. "Yes, sorry. I was just thinking about the mile-long to-do list I have," I replied as smoothly as I could.

I bristled at the idea that even though I was innocent from the real crime here, I wasn't completely off the hook. Even if I didn't do what I did to get rid of the evidence of my powers, I had a feeling he'd still feel the same. Hardly fair of him, really.

"Thank you for stopping by, sir. Like I said before, I'll certainly let you know if I find out anything that might help you all," I said sweetly, ready to be rid of the man. It wasn't anything too personal but having him in here was only making my mind race.

"I thank you kindly for that. Have a good evening, Miss Devaine." He left through the back door out to the cemetery, stopping to check out a few of the gravestones with interest.

I practically held my breath until I saw him take off in his cruiser back down the side road.

I don't know how long I was standing there on the back porch, but at some point it started to rain. The light drizzle splashed on the worn porch railing, sneaking in through the bits of screen that were torn and frayed.

My heart finally calmed down a bit, but I was still anxious. That was a little too close for comfort and with the sheriff's eye on me and what I was doing, I had even more of a cause for concern.

I clutched at the necklace dangling from my throat. Upstairs, heavy footsteps fell across the floor of my bedroom.

Goosebumps pricked across my skin bit by bit as the rain came down in torrents, and I stared across the cemetery to the sliver of Willa-Mae's house that I could see from where I was standing.

How in the world could I have stood there chatting through her being murdered not fifty yards from the side of my house? Right under my very nose? It just didn't make any sense. I didn't have the psychic sense that many of the witches out there did, but I felt as though the sudden, violent change in the energy around me should've done something. What was I missing?

Regardless of what Sheriff Paine thought of me, I should've been paying more attention to making sure the real killer was found.

Because I certainly wasn't a fan of all this attention on me.

14
CRACKING THE CASE

The days dragged on with the rain leaving everything soggy and bleak. I had plenty to do, but a break to unwind was what I really needed. After all, if I was going to leave the bright lights and busyness of Vegas, I was going to need something to help fill that hole.

Well, maybe not fill in all of it. I was pretty content with the peace and quiet I got—aside from Grifter coming in and out and generally everywhere I went until he was bored with me.

That's what I was. Bored. The idea sounded preposterous —I couldn't remember the last time I was genuinely bored. Being a witch certainly helped prevent it. What I needed was something mundane to keep my mind from having to work too hard.

It took some doing, but I loaded the used flat screen TV into the back of my old Mercedes and thanked the young couple. Their yard sale got rained out, so they were practically giving things away. Bless that rain, as my Grandmother always said.

Everything was plugged in by nightfall. I turned out the lights and let myself sink into the couch that Frannie offered to me for free. I flipped through the channels until something caught my eye. I wasn't planning to watch the news—that would have the exact opposite effect on me. But it was hard to look away when I saw two correspondents talking on air with the headline 'Witches Everywhere—What Does This All Mean?'

Oh, I really shouldn't be watching this. It's just going to upset me…

This was one of those rare times I didn't listen to my brain and instead, sat back with my eyes glues to the television.

The one news anchor was in the studio while they had a guest on the show—apparently a witch from Salem, Massachusetts of all places. I clucked my tongue. Talk about cliché.

The witch was really playing up her part—dark makeup, many silver bits hanging from her face and ears. She even wore a black floppy witch hat as if she wanted to make extra sure everyone knew exactly what she was. Wouldn't it have been something if she wasn't even a true witch?

Most witches I've ever come in contact with were just as normal and everyday as I was—with the exception of my own family, of course. Grandmother and my Aunties had an air of superiority to them when it came to normal people. If you didn't have the magic in your bloodline then they didn't want to have much to do with you unless you had the coin to pay for their time.

"There's no need to be scared of us. We use our abilities for good, only," the neophyte witch said, her eyes flashing.

Both the anchorwoman and the correspondent had frowns on their faces.

The correspondent's eyes narrowed. "What about curses?"

The witch just laughed. "Oh, those. Just fairytales—there's no such thing as a real curse. Unless you count taxes."

That got a good, if not uneasy chuckle out of the other two.

"You see that, Grifter? If they're going to interview a witch, oughtn't they find a real one of us? Curses aren't real —ha! Tell that to my mother."

Grifter, who was lying at my feet, lifted his head to look at me, cocking his head to the side.

"I'll have you know that curses are very real. Only the most powerful of us can cast a curse that can do much damage. And you better believe there have been plenty of witches and warlocks who have used this to their benefit—warlocks especially. They're much rarer and for a reason. I've always reckoned that it was because men tend to be more power-hungry as it is."

I sighed, realizing there was no point in giving Grifter the third-degree about the patriarchy, and I changed the channel.

Finally a show to relax to. I leaned back and brought my feet under me. The Real Housewives were all driving through the desert in a convertible, their long manes of hair spreading out behind them. The last desert reminded me of something.

The Real Housewives of Vegas flashed across the screen and I understood. I'd seen those distant dusty mountains and the flat desert plains enough to recognize them, and a sort of funny homesickness welled up inside of me.

Vegas had been my home for over five years. I didn't have any plans on moving away from it any time soon. I frowned at the TV and the women with their designer clothes and their fruity cocktails by the pool.

I was forced to leave the life I loved because of the High-Order's rather rash decision to come out publicly to the world and even though it wasn't so obvious to anyone that I was a witch, it did put an extra target on my back. Especially after I ditched the rest of the tour. People were actually looking for me, or at least the younger version of myself they all knew, according to Corinne.

She continued to be the saint that she's always been, calling me up a few times a week to check in with me and make sure I was taking care of myself.

Truth be told, I wasn't sure how to answer her. Try as I might, it was hard to keep the murder off my mind. The sheriff's department didn't seem any closer to finding out what really happened that night—and it made it all the more difficult to get a good decent night's sleep.

The housewives were doing their trash-talking confessionals to the camera and I tried to focus on what they were saying. I had no idea who was who and what they did.

"Lordy, boy, I don't know how these women have the energy to put toward fussing with one another. It's exhausting just to listen to them." I reached down to scratch the top of Grifter's head.

The more I tried to lose myself in the pettiness of these women, the more my mind wandered. I thought about the day I met Geena's friends at Bubba-Rays. How friendly they had (mostly) been. Those were true friends right there—none of this trashy mess you always see on television nowadays.

Geena was such a kind woman for bringing me into her little circle. She's already been by to chat with me twice since then. It made me mad that the first occasion had been interrupted by that social deviant.

Everything about Gus set my teeth on edge. Men like him thought they could carry on like some kind of uncouth Neanderthal, which was possibly my least favorite type of person.

He'd purposefully sought to irritate us. Then there was the way he referred to Willa-Mae as an 'old hag.' She may not have given many a reason to like her, but that felt like overkill. It felt like there was some real malice behind his words…

If he worked in the morgue like Geena had told me, then wouldn't it be possible for him to somehow fudge the medical records? Make it seem like it was the obvious thing that killed her when really it was something else?

Then again, maybe she was strangled—Sheriff Paine seemed to think that was the case. And really, how could someone fake that?

I sat upright, accidentally bumping my legs into Grifter. He let out a soft growl and lazily got up to go lie on the opposite side of the room.

"I'm sorry, boy. It's just the wheels turning in my head..." I stood with my hands on my hips and began pacing the length of my sitting room. It would be only too easy for someone his size to strangle a somewhat frail older woman. And TJ did say that Gus used to be on the wrestling team in school...which would make it even easier.

Gus Barnaby came across as a real snake in the grass, even to someone new in town like me. He didn't much care for first impressions. What if there was something to this theory after all?

What if Gus was Willa-Mae's killer?

15

BEIGNETS TO DIE FOR

The first rule of following someone? Blend into the background.

My red and white striped umbrella and black trench coat weren't exactly doing me favors with my spying endeavors, but it was all I had to work with.

Now, I wasn't the nosy type of person but the way I saw it, this wasn't me being nosy—this was me assisting the sheriff's department. In my own way.

Thanks to some snooping around the internet, I was able to find the neighborhood Gus lived in and with the helpful clue about his truck unknowingly given to me by Frannie, I knew he drove a big and loud jacked-up black pickup.

It didn't take me long to pick his house out in the small neighborhood. It was pulled up in the yard of a dingy rancher, with a big pair of brass ones hanging from the tailgate. Oh yes. This was definitely Gus's place.

I knew sneaking around and following him wasn't my brightest idea to date, but I needed to know my suspicions were unfounded.

An hour after I pulled up to park in the street the door to

the rancher opened and out came Gus with a beer in hand. He chugged whatever was left before tossing it into the over-flowing trashcan beside his house. He jumped up into the truck and powered it up, the loud rumble of his engine tangible even in my chest.

How could Gregory and I have not heard that loud thing pull up into the side street by the cemetery that night? This was one of the pinch-points in my theory.

I waited until he was halfway down the street before I threw my car into drive and followed far behind him.

First there was the trip to the gas station. That was straight-forward—he went in to pay for his gas and brought out another twelve-pack of beer just to shove into the bed of the truck.

Keeping a good distance between the two of us, I waited until he was back on the road and heading downtown. When he turned left at the stoplight before the town square, I hurried to keep up, nearly running the red light. I winced as I glanced around to make sure no one else saw.

The black pick-up slowed down along the street before Gus parallel parked it outside the barber shop. For someone with a pretty shiny bald head, I was surprised to see him… oh.

He sidestepped the barber shop and headed into the next business down. A sign with a bright green macaron and fork hung from the shop. The pretty scripted words on the shop's front window read, 'The Macaroon Boutique.'

"Well, I'll be darned. So you've got a sweet tooth, do you?" I murmured and I parked across the street. I'd been meaning to stop into Cinda's bakery, anyway.

This would give me the *perfect* excuse for spying on him.

I took my time striding into the bakery, careful to shake off the rain from my umbrella before I went inside. The sweet air was like a gentle breeze, hitting me softly but strongly all at once. There was a deep-fried deliciousness to it, and I could almost taste the powdered sugar on my lips.

Forgetting about Gus for a moment, I found myself walking toward the front to where there was a long glass encasement full of the brightest and fluffiest macarons I'd ever seen. Not only those, but all sorts of different baked goods lines the three shelves along it. Fruity fritters, tasty turnovers, mini pies in cute little tins, both large and small muffins depending on what you were in the mood for—and oh my. My personal favorite.

It would be extremely unladylike to drool in front of anyone, so I swallowed against the taste in my mouth. Beignets, freshly powdered with sugar, too. Little puffs of steam were coming out of the batch of them, frosting the glass they were underneath.

"I was wondering when you'd stop by."

I looked up to see Cinda, wearing a bright green apron with her name in curly white letters on it. She smiled at me and nodded to the beignets. "Maman was born in New Orleans—she's Cajun. She showed me the proper way to make them there. Some people like to use steam but I'm a yeast girl, myself. And I ground down the sugar myself. Gives it that extra oomph."

"Lord, Cinda. I walked in here thinking I was going to get a snack, not an assortment of heaven. This place is so cozy, and it smells like... like my dreams," I laughed.

Cinda chuckled along, tapping her finger against the glass counter. "If I may? I recommend trying the beignets while they're still hot. Then you can refresh your palette with one of the macarons. Or two. I wouldn't want you to limit yourself."

"I don't know that my waistline agrees." I winked at her as she pulled out the tray loaded with the pillowy treats on it.

"Remember I did say something about a free sample to new customers..."

I watched her load one of the beignets onto a pink and green napkin and slide it over to me with a cheeky grin.

"They say that a friend's cookin' slides right off the thighs, so no worries there, sugar."

Friend. It was not something many had referred to me as, and it came so easily from Cinda. My chest constricted as I took the beignet and gave her a quiet thank you.

The sweet yet buttery and savory dough mixed with just the right amount of fresh powdered sugar was to die for—I could imagine them serving these bad boys up in heaven on a puffy little cloud it was so delectable. I dabbed at the corner of my mouth once I was finished, wishing there was more.

"I see why you're the boss lady here. That was the most delicious beignet I've ever had! And I lived in New Orleans for ten years at one point. But don't tell them at Bayou Boogaloo's about that. I'd never hear the end of it," I said, flashing her the biggest smile. Not just for the food, for the pure kindness she'd shown me already.

"Don't mention it. I haven't been down there myself in so long I wouldn't know a Bayou Boogaloo from a Jumbo Gumbo. So what brings you here, anyway? Were you just stopping by for some conversation? I plan on taking a break here shortly, if you want to wait. Sasha will hold down the fort."

Behind her, a short and frizzy-haired woman with big hazel eyes stared at me through her red-rimmed glasses. She couldn't have been older than twenty-five. I waved back.

What was I going to tell her? Suddenly I realized that I hadn't even been paying attention to the whole reason I was here, and I glanced over my shoulder, relieved to see Gus sitting across from some other guy who was facing away from me. At least he hadn't left yet.

"Oh, you know. Just happened to be in the neighborhood."

"It's wetter than an otter's pocket out there. I wouldn't be running about if I were you. As much as I hate to say it, Maman was right about catching a cold in this kind of weather."

I nodded. "It is the season for it, that is true. I've been dosing up on plenty of vitamin C and elderberry syrup just in case." Plus the charmed lavender tea and shot of magic-burst potion, but I left that part out.

"Smart girl. Would you like a drink? Maybe a small bag of those?"

I glanced up to the quaint chalkboard above her head and scanned the menu.

"Hm. I think I'll go with a sweet tea with lemon and try some of those macarons of yours. How about one raspberry and one chocolate?" It was embarrassing just how much my mouth was already watering.

She was half-way through putting them into the bag for me before I was even finished. "Call it a hunch. I had a feeling you were a raspberry and chocolate kind of gal."

I raised a brow. Sometimes non-witches threw me for a loop with their intuition. "How so?"

She gestured up and down to me before turning and pouring me some sweet tea. "You're a classic— a classy gal who likes to be swept off her feet, who carries herself with poise and self-assurance. Is polite and genuine but doesn't take heehaw from anyone. I almost went strawberry, but you mentioned how your favorite was raspberry at Bubba-Rays."

I took the drink. "Well, now. That's an oddly accurate description. You sure you aren't a mind-reader?"

Cinda gave the kind of hearty laugh that rattled your bones. "Me? Ha! Hardly, sugar. I'm no witchy woman, as much as I wish I could claim to be."

Did I dare? I didn't want to suddenly feel put out by her ill-fated feelings on us, but I couldn't help myself. "Oh?

And... why would you want to claim to be a witch? Everyone else seems worried about them, wouldn't you say?"

She nodded. "Well, people get scared of their own shadow if it talked back to 'em. They don't like what they don't understand, even if there's no reason to fear it." With another shrug, she started untying her apron. "I like to reserve my judgment for when I actually need it. Go ahead and grab yourself a chair. I'll be done shortly. I hear the boss is a real stickler for taking breaks." She winked again and patted the counter.

As silly as it felt, my heart was singing. Cinda was truly a good person through and through. It didn't mean I was going to be shouting the truth from her rooftop, but at least I knew I could count her in my corner if the need ever did arise.

The corner of the little bakery seating area was a perfect vantage point to keep an eye on Gus. I cozied up into the booth and pretended to be thoroughly interested in my macarons. Oh fine, I wasn't pretending— they were just as delicious as I'd hoped. But I still had my eye on Gus.

He was busy going back and forth with the man sitting across from him, whatever their exchange was must have been a serious one. Gus's expression was one of apprehension.

Hm. Maybe I should have sat closer after all.

It clicked in my head the moment the other man turned to reach down into the briefcase he had at his feet, that I recognized him. Barnaby. Gregory Barnaby.

How had I not put two and two together? Maybe it was because Gus and Gregory were so different that it seemed almost impossible for them to be related. And judging from their casualness with each other, despite the argument, they looked like they might be cousins, maybe even brothers.

Well now, Birdie. You can't go assuming someone is a product of their family. Look at you. You're about as far from Vivienne and Lilian as can be. And good on that.

"Birdie! Fancy seeing you here." Frannie was coming from the deluge outside, immediately pushing back her plastic haircap to reveal a perfectly coiffed updo. There were two things I'd always been envious of as a witch; those who could levitate, and those who could perform true glamour magic. I could only make people believe things to an extent, but to be able to poof my hair into the exact color and style I'd like whenever I wanted? Now that was some good magic.

"Looks like you got caught up in it out there," I said, smiling as she took a seat at the table.

"Did I ever! I'm already looking forward to the drier air. All the humidity does a number on my hair. And I simply can't expect my clients to come back if I can't even take care of my own mop top. Ooh, what do you have there?"

I shook my drink. "Sugar rush in a cup. Sweet tea," added in between sips, "but so, so good. My grandmother made hers so bitter. I'm always happy to find a good tea."

"I'm always popping in over here to have Cinda refill our pitcher at the salon—oh yes, we have our own pitcher," she added before I had a chance to even question it. Not that I would, of course. Any southern woman worth her weight in grits knew the value of some good tea.

She went up to Sasha at the front and ordered her own tea and a ham and cheese croissant before settling back into her seat and checking her face in the mirror. "Oh fiddlesticks. This lipstick is no good. I don't see what all those young women on the Instagram say, this matte look is not my favorite. What do you think, Birdie?" She puckered her coral-colored lips at me.

"If you find a good formula then you'd be doing yourself a favor. I love mine. Whenever I would do my show... that is, my presentations... at my job... before I was, er, retired... I would use them all the time. They stay put, and if you find a good one, it won't look so dried out. The color is beautiful on you though, dear."

Oh my word, that was about as smooth as a gator's back. The only thing I had really let on about regarding my past was the traveling I've done, and a couple of the jobs I've held. Not exactly lies, but more omissions.

She looked in the compact mirror again, nodding. "Maybe you're right."

We chatted for a few more minutes about Frannie's last client who came in with a badly done home-perm, when Cinda finally sat down.

"Tell me why I had Saint Peter's call me just now, asking for a two-hundred count order of three different flavored macarons, after I've just spent the last two nights getting caught up on their order of three different flavored macarons?"

Frannie and I exchanged a look. "So they just called to remind you?"

"Oh-ho. No. They wanted macarons to begin with, but the silly girl who called the first time around ordered coconut macaroons. Two totally different things. Now I have to bust my can of biscuits just to get it done in time."

I let out a low whistle. I'd offer but I'm no whiz at the baking thing.

Across the way, the conversation between Gus and Gregory picked up. My ears pricked as I tried to listen in while still commiserating with poor Cinda.

"I'll take you on anytime Greg. I whooped you then, I'll whoop you now." There was a jovial tone in Gus's words. "State champion versus what, three-time county champion? Is that even worth all the breath it took to say?"

Gregory shoved at Gus playfully. "Oh shut up. At least Mom came to my meets."

Gus just rolled his eyes, shoving a fistful of his food into his mouth. Why did he remind me so much of a darn gorilla?

"You're thinking so hard that there's steam coming out of

your ears, girl. Everything all right?" Cinda's words cut through my concentration like a knife.

I blinked. "Oh. Not at all. I'm just… surprised." I leaned in when she frowned. "I didn't realize that Gregory was Gus's brother."

Frannie and Cinda both nodded, obviously understanding. "I know it. They're like night and day, aren't they? Gregory was your realtor, right? He turned out better than Gus did, that's for sure. He helped Ruby and Shawn find their house if I'm not mistaken.

"Yeah, well I didn't lose money on a bingo game, did I, little bro?"

I looked past Cinda, distracted again.

There was a change to Gregory's body language—he tensed up. "Nah. I'm not letting you get a rise out of me that easily."

I was sort of proud of him. It couldn't be easy being related to someone like Gus. A potential killer, even.

A hand waved in front of me and I blushed hard. "Sorry," I replied as Frannie and Cinda tried to get my attention again. "It just makes me wonder if Gregory knows…"

"Knows what, sugar?" Cinda asked.

I bit my lip. Cinda did just call me her friend… And I felt I could trust Frannie just as much. And neither of them were friends of Gus's. It didn't matter that he was Gregory's brother. Gus was not innocent in this, I just knew it.

I leaned closer to whisper. "I don't want to alarm you, but I think I might know who killed Willa-Mae."

Cinda's eyes went wide. There was no mistaking her intrigue. "Who?"

Now I just felt silly for even saying it out loud. But there was no going back, so I dropped my voice even lower. "Gus."

While Frannie gasped, Cinda squinted her eyes. "What? I'm sorry hun, I didn't catch that."

"Gus," I whispered a little louder, nodding my chin in his direction.

I don't know what kind of reaction I expected from her, but it wasn't this. She frowned for a moment, looked at Frannie, then cracked a smile. "That useless bag of bones? If dumb were dirt, he'd be about an acre. He don't have the kind of brains for that operation."

"But, well, I understand he seems a little *inept* for carrying out something like this without getting caught. But I have my reasons for thinking it's him."

Cinda crossed her legs. "Birdie. Are you telling me you have proof?"

All right, so now I felt really silly. All I had were hunches to go on—super sleuth I was not. "I saw him earlier with a beer in his hand, getting into his truck. And he went to pick up another twelve-pack."

"How did you know..." she gasped, a funny little half-disbelief chuckle bubbling up out of her. "Were you following him?"

My cheeks reddened but kept going. "Ruby told me that Willa-Mae's body reeked of alcohol. He could've been drunk. He could've been drunk and mad and took it out on her. And," I said, the words tumbling out of my mouth in a hurry, "TJ did say he was on the wrestling team in school, right? I'd bet my bottom dollar he knows just how to put someone in a chokehold to suffocate them. She was strangled, after all. And his attitude about Willa-Mae wasn't exactly cordial, was it?"

Frannie took my hands in hers and I was vaguely aware of her pretty coral nails to match her lips. "It couldn't have been him."

I tilted my head to the side as if it would change what she'd already said. "How do you know that?"

"It was poker night. Harry was hosting that night, and the fellas didn't leave until mid-way through the night. I know because I missed out on plenty of beauty sleep because of all the ruckus downstairs, mind you. Gus was there at the poker game, too. Harry told me the next day that Gus took quite a bit home, too. So he was there when Willa-Mae was… well, you know," she dropped her voice, "killed."

The bottom of my stomach dropped to my feet. "Oh."

Well. Was I back to square one, or what?

16

IT'S MAGIC

My shoulders slumped. I didn't want to peg an innocent man as a killer… even if he was a nasty person. Yet here I was, doing exactly that.

"Don't look too disappointed," Cinda joked, sounding a little uneasy. "It's an honest mistake, sugar."

I did my best to brush it off as if it were nothing. But my glassy eyes told them another story. I was quick to turn away before I sat there blubbering like a baby, but Frannie took my hand and squeezed.

"There, there. I know you must be worried about the person who did… *that terrible thing*… being out there still. If you'd like, Birdie, I can have Harry send one of his deputies out to keep an eye on the place for a little longer."

But I waved her off, sniffling, and dreading how much I was ruining my mascara. "No, that's all right. I can't just stay on guard the rest of my life. I have a house to renovate, after all. It's just that I thought I had it right—my instinct is almost always right." I cut myself off, embarrassed at how preposterous that must have sounded. They were probably wondering, 'who does this woman think she is?'

Frannie stood up, claiming she needed a bathroom break,

leaving me and Cinda there staring at each other. My cheeks burned.

"I swear I'm not crazy," I said, doing my best to sound lighthearted about it. It was harder than it sounded.

"None of that, now. No one thinks you're crazy. You made some darn good points, even if they were only coincidences. You're very observant, you know that?"

That wasn't the first time I'd heard that. "It doesn't matter. Cinda, I—where are your napkins?" I asked, searching the room. Crying in front of another woman was one thing, but I was *not* about to have snot streaming out of my nose on top of it. I had a little bit more dignity than all *that*.

She pointed to the counter that ran along one of the walls. "All the way to the right."

I thanked her and as elegantly as possible, covered my nose and rushed over to clean myself up. Thankfully the bakery wasn't too crowded. No one was paying attention to me as I stood with my back to everyone, feeling lower than a snake in the mud.

The squeak of metal chairs against the floor made me look back over my shoulder. I whipped my head back, nearly holding my breath as Gregory and Gus got up to leave.

"Catch you later little bro. And remember what I said," Gus said, his tone not matching the casual words.

The tension between them was still there, but apparently Gregory wasn't much affected by it. "See you later, then," he replied. He, on the other hand, sounded practically indifferent. I'd never understand sibling relationships…

I held still as I heard Gus walk past me, and out of the corner of my eye I could see him walking past the front window and into the rain.

Wonder what they were talking about? Regardless of him being innocent in my personal game of Clue, Gus couldn't be an easy person to be related to. I frowned.

I needed to stay out of their business and worry about my own.

"I was wondering when you were going to come scoop up your next box. Business must be booming for you, huh? You've already been in here four times this month!" Cinda's voice boomed.

I threw the napkin in the trash, hoping for the best. Coincidently, I'd forgotten to bring my own compact to check my face with.

"Something like that," I heard Gregory say. He was standing at the front counter where Cinda was now back behind.

"Well I'm plum-pickin' happy for you, Greg. Don't forget about us little people when you go on to sell million-dollar homes in the future," Cinda joked, sliding a medium-sized white box toward him. "The usual?"

Gregory sighed. "I wish. But my client isn't a fan of *the usual*—he's allergic to flour and almonds or something."

"That poor soul," Cinda said.

Gregory nodded and pulled out his wallet. "I want to make sure he's satisfied with his housewarming gift. Maybe we could go with some of your macarons? They don't have any flour in them, do they?"

"They may not have any wheat flour in them, sweetie, but they do have almond flour in them, which wouldn't be any better. I do happen to have some flourless dark chocolate cookies. They've been selling like hotcakes with the Keto crowd. Would that work?"

"Perfect. I'll take a dozen," he said, sounding full of relief.

She got to work sorting the cookies out and placing them in a smaller box while I took a seat at the table, waiting for Frannie still.

"I hold a monthly baking class, if you're ever interested in it. Maybe then you can learn the ways of a master chef, and you can make your own treats for your clients," Cinda said as she took out some plastic wrap and dressed up the white box of cookies, tying bits of ribbon around it.

"Mm, probably not the best idea. I'm terrible at baking."

I raised a brow, still turned away from the rest of the bakery as Gregory laughed at something else Cinda said.

"Not even a single cookie, no. I am oddly fantastic at burning things in the kitchen."

Frannie returned just as he thanked Cinda and walked out the front door of the shop.

"What are your plans for the rest of the day?" Frannie spoke up as soon as she sat down.

I shook my head. Without having the need of following Gus around today, it felt like I'd wasted one good day for something pointless. "I'm honestly not quite sure."

Something was percolating in the back of my mind, but I held my tongue.

"This weather is really putting a damper on my mood. I had plans to work in my garden after I got home, but that's down the drain."

Cinda took a seat again at the table, this time with her own cup of sweet tea. "You better now?"

"Me? Oh. Yes, I suppose I am. I'm just—" but I cut myself off. I was going to keep my thoughts to myself because I was being silly yet again.

"Just what, sugar?"

Oh, to heck with it. "I think Gregory might have lied to me."

Cinda's eyes went wide as she took a sip of her tea. "About what? Surely everything is sound with the house?"

I was already wanting to backtrack. Why in the world did you open your mouth, you silly girl? "No, no. It's nothing like that. It's small, really. I shouldn't be fussing about it."

Frannie and Cinda both pursed their lips at me. I should've just kept my mouth shut. But there was no use, now.

"He did that for me. Brought me a cake. He said he made it for me."

Cinda squinted at me. "I'm not following."

"He just told you he's—oh, it really doesn't matter," I said, cutting myself off. I was of half a mind to just take my leave before I made matters worse.

"He lied about the cake?" Frannie guessed.

"It wasn't a big deal at the time. He told me he made the rum cake himself, but then he told Cinda just now that he's a terrible baker."

"Can't really blame him too much for that. Maybe he wants to come off as more caring with his clients. A home-baked good sounds better and more genuine than bringing something store-bought. Or at least he might think so," Cinda said. "I'm not a fan of someone trying to pass on my food as their own, mind you, but it isn't much more than a little white lie, don't you think?"

I sighed. "You have a point. I don't know… I think I'm just a little jittery lately. I'm not usually so suspicious of people."

Lately it's becoming more and more of a habit, though. I can't go turning into one of the recluses who never see the light of day.

I wanted to believe in Gregory. After all, he was so wonderful to push through for the house for me, and he'd never given me any real reason to think otherwise. And the more I sat and thought about it, the worse I felt.

"Ladies, I'd love to stay and chat longer, but I think I'd like to go home and lie down for a little while. The weather is putting a hurting on my spirits, I think."

I didn't want to push any buttons—it was clear Cinda thought nothing of Gregory's supposed white lie to me. She was probably right, and I was just overreacting after leaning so far in the wrong section on with his brother.

It dawned on me that I had something up my sleeve that I've been ignoring this whole time—magic.

On my way out, I fished the mini version of my spellbook from my purse, glad to see that the rain had finally decided to shut off for a while. With the exception of a few cars passing by Porter Street was nearly empty, thanks to the rain.

I wasn't the best when it came down to potions. I did well enough to squeak on by with the basic things. But a truth spell? That was not something to take lightly.

Leaning against the bricked wall that separated Cinda's bakery from the barber shop, I flipped through the pages until I found exactly what I was looking for.

"Truth-Obtaining Potion. Oh my, there are more ingredients here than I thought there'd be," I said quietly to myself, frowning. Half of the things would need to be bought, and the potion needed to brew for three days straight. I wasn't exactly prone to sitting in the kitchen to begin with, but to stir a potion for three days straight? No, ma'am.

I tucked the book back into my purse just as it started pouring again. Go figure. My luck these days, I swear.

Opening my striped umbrella, I groaned. Maybe if I just did a little bit of shield magic… Voila! The umbrella repelled the rain, keeping a good foot of dry air all around me as I started walking to my car. My fingers buzzed with bright bits of electricity—which usually meant I had too much built-up magical energy in me to begin with. I couldn't remember the last time that had happened to me.

I blew the blue sparks off my fingers.

And ran right into Geena.

17
LOVELY SHADE OF GREEN

The world stopped. I slowly became aware that I was holding my breath. I let it out and struggled to take in another.

"Oh my God," Geena gasped, blinking down at the hand I was still holding by my face. "Oh! Geena Louise, watch your mouth!" Geena whispered to herself in a rush automatically, as if it were something she'd said a thousand times before.

Her eyes refused to look elsewhere other than my hand. I lowered it to my side slowly, hoping against all hope that there was a way I could explain this all away.

But the words never came.

Finally coming to her senses, Geena pulled at my coat. I swatted her hand away out of instinct, my blood pumping through my veins like thick tar moving through a straw. What did she think she was doing? My mind didn't want to comprehend the idea of my friend wanting to do me any harm.

But she yanked at my trench coat's arm again anyway, directing me to follow her until we were well out of sight. She waited until the trash truck finished dumping the contents of the green dumpster into the back of it and was on its way, before saying a word.

"Birdie. Tell me what it was that I just saw. I need to know that I'm not suddenly developing cataracts or something," she said, rather nervously before adding in a long exhale, "and they run on my Mama's side so it's possible. And I'm too young for all that so I'm pretty sure that's not it."

A small bit of relief helped me calm down some, but after I realized she wasn't about to try and throw me to the dogs, I frowned. How in the world was I supposed to explain this? And how dumb did I have to be for not having a backup plan in case something like this happened? I must have been in total denial, thinking I was out of danger of being found out… Because I most certainly had no idea what to say.

Geena cleared her throat. "Maybe… maybe you're just scared." She still looked spooked, but I couldn't blame her for it.

And she wasn't exactly wrong, either.

Geena took a deep breath in and let it out. "Birdie. Before you say anything, please understand that I'm not going to tell a soul about… well, whatever that was." Even though she just dragged me around the back of the shopping center, she hesitated at taking my hand in hers. Maybe she thought I would electrocute her or something.

I bit down on my lip, hard. I knew I wasn't exactly an animal trapped in a cage. Geena wasn't keeping me here—I knew that. But I still felt a twisting sort of obligation to explain myself. Even though I really, really didn't want to.

"I… don't know what to say," I said softly, unable to meet her gaze.

She nodded. "Then let me go first for a minute. Whatever you are, whatever you can do, I know you're still a good person. I can feel it in my gut. I have a sense for these things, you know," she said, finally reaching out and squeezing my hand in hers. "Am I wrong?"

"I'd like to think I'm a good person."

Leaning against the brick wall behind us, Geena groaned. "Don't tell nobody, but this is one of those moments I really wish I hadn't quit smoking. I really feel like I need a cigarette."

I don't know why, but it broke the tension just enough. Geena chuckled softly, and looked at me, amused.

"I was never one for them, but I wouldn't turn down a shot of something strong if someone offered," I replied, daring to smile a little. It still felt off, but I could appreciate her trying to lighten the mood.

"How would you like a ride back to my house? If you're okay with that, I mean. I just figure it would be smarter than standing out here and catching a chill."

Geena's home was exactly as I'd pictured it. I'd been outside of it to chit-chat with her and sometimes the other girls, but this was the first time I'd actually been inside it.

The walls were a cream color that was just warm enough without being too yellow, and she had carpet throughout the living room, which she immediately apologized for when I sat down on her couch.

"One of these days I'll have the darn carpet tore up and taken out. We used to have a dog when Ruby was a little girl, and try as I might, it still smells like the dog in here when it gets really muggy outside. The Hampton House has nice original floors, doesn't it?"

I nodded, sipping the steaming cup of chamomile tea Geena made for me. "It does. The Hamptons had an old varnish on the floors that I'm working on updating. I have to sand down the floors in order to do it, though. But there's a slew of things I need to do before I get to that point first."

Glancing around the room, it was hard not to notice all of the photos that were hanging up or placed everywhere. Most of Ruby, plenty of Max and Eva, and some of Ruby and Shawn's wedding day. A huge portrait of Ruby looking gorgeous as all get-out in her wedding gown as she and Shawn shot in some majestic hallway was hanging over Geena's mantle.

"She gets so embarrassed," she laughed, nodding her chin toward the big picture. "She's always telling me I need new hobbies. You know, instead of taking pictures of her all the time."

My jaw dropped. "You... you took that?"

Her cheeks went red. "Mmhm."

"Well butter my butt and call me a biscuit. You are a mighty fine photographer, Geena! Got any other secret talents hidden up those sleeves?"

The moment it popped out of my mouth I already knew what she was going to come back with.

And she knew I knew. The corners of her mouth curled up. "I suppose I should be asking you the same?"

"Well. We're already here. Might as well get it over with," I mumbled. I thought that maybe if we just beat around the bush for a while longer, she might actually give up.

Geena sat down opposite of me in a recliner. "I don't even know what to ask you. But I guess first thing's first." She squared her shoulders and looked me dead-on. "Are you a witch? Like a real, honest-to-God witch? Like the ones that are all over the news now?"

I looked away for a moment before nodding. "Yes. I'm a witch."

Geena let out a low whistle, and sat back in the recliner, her eyes wide. "That is... Even though I knew you were going to say yes, it's still so odd to actually hear you say it. I don't... I don't suppose you want to tell me about it?"

"What would you like to know?" Was it just me, or did she actually sound sorta excited?

Geena waved me off. "Whatever you'd like to share, really. Have you always been a witch? Is it something you're born with knowing? Or is it something you learn?"

"Well, yes. I've always been a witch. You're born one—it's in your genetics. Passed down by the females in the family."

"Only the females of the family can be witches?"

"We call male witches warlocks. They do exist, but there are far more witches than warlocks. Which is due to the fact that only the female witch can pass down magical ability. When a warlock is born, he is unable to father children, and therefore cannot pass on any magical abilities to his child."

I went on to explain a little more about how the High-Order of Magical Beings worked as our loosely formed governing body on behalf of the witches and wizards of the world. And how frustrated I was when they suddenly announced out of the clear blue sky, that we were walking amongst the normal population now.

"So there was no warning beforehand?" she asked, shocked. "That's not fair at all! What about all of the people who probably needed to make arrangements... I can't even imagine. I'm so sorry, Birdie. They don't sound like the kind of organization that needs to be running anything, if you ask me."

I shrugged. "There's not really much any of us can do about it now. The press conference they gave was all the proof anyone needed. And of course there are the witches and warlocks who see this as a blessing—they've been wanting to be out in the open with their powers. But I know better than that."

"Birdie?"

"Hm?"

Geena hesitated. "I don't want to sound rude, because normally I'd never ask another woman her age but—"

"One hundred and thirty-three. That's one thing I don't mind bragging about, actually," I said. I had to admit, I found a funny sort of satisfaction from seeing the way her mouth dropped open again. It was as if my age was harder to believe than the fact that I was a witch.

"Oh my stars in heaven! Are you for real?"

"Absolutely. I was born in 1886. Actually, I was born in 1886… right here, in Nella." I hadn't been expecting it, but a big weight finally lifted off my shoulders as soon as I admitted it. Finally… someone knows that I'm really just back home after so long. I'm not new in the slightest.

Geena brought her hand to her mouth. "That is really something else. You were born here? In 1886?" she sputtered, trying to wrap her head around it. "What in the…? So you were here growing up? What was it like back then? Oh my goodness, I have so many questions!"

I laughed and sipped some more of my tea. "Might as well sit back. It's a long story…"

And for the next several hours, and in-between a few cups of tea and some leftovers from her fridge, I sat across from Geena, telling her my actual life story. About all three husbands, all the places I'd traveled and lived, why I ran away at fifteen, and why I thought I'd never see Nella again.

By the time I looked up at the cute cuckoo clock Geena had hung up on the wall, the overcast day was turning to night.

I stood up and stretched, surprised at how energized I felt after getting it all out of my system. I couldn't even remember the last time I'd spilled the beans about myself to anyone, much less all of the them.

Geena was busy in the kitchen, washing up our plates. She smacked my hands away when I tried to take over. "So this screening power of yours. How does it work, exactly?"

Now, I'm not the pranking type of gal. But this was an

opportunity that would not present itself again for a long time.

I closed my eyes, imagining the water she had her hands stuck in was not water, but a big sink full of a lovely shade of green Jello, and that the dishes and silverware were floating in the middle of it. As soon as I thought it into existence, Geena shrieked.

"What in the H-E-Double Hockey Sticks!?" She yanked her arms backward and nearly tumbled right into me.

I giggled. "It works a little something like that, hun."

Geena, who needed a moment to realize that she wasn't actually washing dishes in a sink of green Jello, stuck out her tongue at me. "All right, all right. Next time I should probably be more careful before I ask you how to do your magic."

"I had to. I can't remember the last time I got to do that to someone who actually knew it wasn't real."

There was a pause before she tilted her head and looked at me carefully. "Have you had to use your powers on people often?"

I looked away. "Well, I mean, that's how I got away with my shows in Vegas."

She nodded, chuckling to herself. "I still can't believe you're that Birdie. Lordy, if Harry Paine knew, he'd hit the ceiling!"

I raised a brow, taking one of the plates she'd rinsed and drying it off with the nearby dishtowel. "Why's that?"

She fixed a big grin at me. "He's a big fan of yours, that's why! Harry's been going on and on to poor Frannie about how badly he wants to go to one of your magic shows. It used to irritate the mess out of her. Not that you need to worry," she quickly added, seeing the look on my face. "You know I won't say a word."

Something about the idea of Sheriff Paine being a big fan of my alter-ego was really throwing me for a loop. "I don't know how to feel about that."

She finished up in the kitchen and we talked some more about Ruby and the grand babies. Geena took out a couple of photo albums from when Ruby was little, and of course I sat there and ooh-ed and ahh-ed over all the pictures.

I couldn't believe just how talented Geena was at capturing all the perfect moments. It was no wonder she had so many pictures up on her walls.

By the time I was at her door and pulling on my trench coat, Geena sighed.

"You're a pretty amazing person, Birdie. I know this is all between the two of us, but I just wish Ruby and girls knew it too. I know you didn't do it on purpose, but I'm so happy I'm lucky enough to know."

That was the last thing I was expecting from her. I made to wipe at my face, hurrying so that she couldn't see the tears welling up in my eyes. I didn't know whether I was just so darn relieved at how it all turned out so far, or if I was terrified that this would still find a way to blow up in my face.

The jury was still out. For now.

18

NOT SO FAST

The bookcase stared at me. I stared right back.

"Don't make me do it. Because I will do it, believe you me."

I took in the jagged bits of the shelves that still remained of the built-in, and sighed. All my life I thought I would live in a house with beautiful built-in bookcases that spanned the entire length of a wall.

This? This was not what I had in mind.

It looked as though at one point in time, someone thought it was best to smash up the bookcases in the study, not with something as big and wieldy as a baseball bat but more of the likes of a hammer. Small but powerful. The splintered shelves that remained were in utter disrepair.

But still, I hated the idea of taking out a once-gorgeous original to the house feature. Especially the bookcase. It only went across one long wall, where in the center, was a small fireplace that was in desperate need of a flue-cleaning.

"I'll come back for you later. I have bigger fish to fry," I said, pointing my finger at the sad-looking thing.

There were so many things to do, that every time I struck something off my list—which was now roughly a mile long—

it was soon after replaced with three more things. It was enough to make me want to shove my head through the half-demo'ed wall.

I walked back downstairs, with Grifter not far behind me. He'd taken up to following me anytime I left a room now. It took me several tries, keeping him out of the bathroom whenever nature was calling.

"Go on now, get! Or I'm going to change your name to something worse!" I'd yelled at him until he skulked back out of the bathroom with his tail between his legs. Of course I'd ended up giving him extra ear scratches afterwards.

The list on the fridge seemed to be pulling me toward it, and I stood with my back against the cool metal, reading over it for the fourth time today.

Franklin and Nathan had finished the rewiring for both levels, thankfully. I even treated them to an extra gift card to, that's right, Olive Garden. I'd overheard Franklin mentioning it to his son when they were leaving for a lunch break one day. He was pretty tickled when I handed him the little envelope.

Ever since I came home yesterday evening from Geena's house, my mind refused to relax. And my body wasn't really cooperating either. I've been pacing back and forth just itching for something to do, and since there were so many things to get done, frustration was starting to build and build in me.

I couldn't very well work on painting until the inspector came back out to check the electrical again. Not to mention all the wall repairs I needed on most of the walls.

Yet paint colors were on my mind. They were easy and fun and didn't require as much from me. I imagined the walls of the kitchen a luscious wine color—intense and sensual. The walls seemed to melt into the very color, the light coming from the windows and the back door hitting them strikingly.

"Hm. That might be too much. I'll save it for another room."

In my head the wine color was replaced with a cheerful chiffon yellow color. I opened my eyes and immediately closed them again.

"Nope, nope, nope. That won't cut it."

Grifter whined at my knees, startling me. "You're like a ninja," I said softly to him, barely having to reach down in order to pat his huge head. "And I need to focus all my energy doing something before I start going crazy."

The paint debate would have to wait for another day.

"I think I know exactly what I need…" I yanked open the fridge and pulled out the bottle of sauvignon blanc I had stashed in the back. It was already half-empty, so I poured myself a sizable glass and sat at the small round table, looking out past the back door.

I was two glasses of wine and a bowl of my favorite grits in, when Grifter, who had been lying by my feet in front of the couch, lifted his head and began to growl.

I nudged him with my knee. "Shh, boy. I need to know if she and the cute cop are going to kiss. They're so close to the mistletoe, they just might." No one interrupted my holiday rom-com binges. No one.

But that didn't stop him, and when he slowly rose to his feet I frowned. "What are you growling at?"

There wasn't much that could scare me, especially after all the things I'd seen in my day. Still, I didn't like the way he kept staring at the hallway where I'd first saw him.

Then I felt it. The chill that sinks down past your spine and crawls all the way back up. The hair on the back on my neck stood on end. I closed my eyes.

Of course. That darn spirit was still here—the one I didn't

have a chance to fully help guide over to the other side. I dropped my head down, wishing I could catch a break.

I knew exactly where it was coming from, too.

The ground was wet with evening dew as I tip-toed across my yard to the cemetery, with my arms full of the ingredients and tools I needed. Yet again.

"Let's get this over with," I muttered under my breath.

There was a flat and cleared piece of the cemetery just along the edge of it—the perfect place to do my bidding. With a keen eye on the little bit of Witch Hazel Lane that I could see, I put down a salt circle about twelve feet in diameter around, situating myself and my things in the middle of it. The wind was blowing more than I'd like, but placed along the circle, the white candles stood against it.

I wished I had brought a sweater with me. The chill locked itself around my spine, and I couldn't stop shivering. Whatever spirit this was, they meant business. And they probably weren't happy at my half-witted attempt to help guide them on last time. A small amount of guilt worked its way through me to anchor me down.

Lighting the match, I sent the flame to each of the other six candles around the circle. The wicks came alive one at a time in little pops of magic until they were all lit and flickering.

"All right. Time to get to it."

The chill picked back up, swirling the leaves against some of the headstones.

And on the air, came another voice.

"Not so fast, Ms. Devaine."

19

A LITTLE TALK

My breath was shallow, but it gave me away as it turned into a thin stream of shivering white as I exhaled.

I was terrified to look, but as I slowly glanced around the circle, I was surprised to see absolutely nothing. *What?*

No one was there. Call it a witch's intuition, but I had a pretty good sense for when people were hiding very close nearby, unseen. And it couldn't be a spirit because it's very rare to a find a corporal enough imprint of a spirit to be able to speak with you so normally.

I'd only come across one once in my life—and it was not a memory I was willing to revisit anytime soon.

"I'm not ready just yet." There it was again, soft, almost like the rustling of the leaves on the ground. But it was definitely *someone*. And there was no doubt about it in my mind that they were speaking directly to me.

I swallowed hard, slowly gathering the one lantern I'd taken inside the circle with me since electronics could interfere. I brought the lantern up closer to my face.

"Hello?"

There was a sigh. "My child. I'm right here."

Not twenty feet away from the outside of the circle of salt, stood a willowy woman beside a tall gravestone.

This wouldn't have shocked me so much if it weren't for the fact that the bottom half of her seemed to blur out of existence.

Sort of like one of my favorite artworks by Gustav Klimt, called 'Love.' Fading into the wind that blew everything around her, the woman clasped her hands together.

"So you can see me. You must be a mystic, after all."

I blew a strand of hair from my face. "Something like that. How…? I just haven't seen a spirit like you in a very long time. Usually you're on a rewind of the moments leading up to your death, without knowing you're dead. Sorry," I quickly added, already screwing this whole thing up. "I don't mean to offend."

She gave me what felt like an appraising look, though I couldn't really be sure. "None taken."

There was an awkward silence as I stood, trying to figure out what to do next. Should I carefully go on with the ritual? What if she turned out to be one of the more heinous spirits? Just because she seemed like a nice gal so far, didn't mean she couldn't go full Exorcist on me.

To test her, I leaned down and began assembling my crystals in the right grid formation, keeping the spirit in my peripheral vision. She didn't move an inch until I stood back up to stretch.

Floating along until she was practically up against the wall of the salt circle, she tilted her head to one side. "If you'd kindly wait, I have some important news for you, Birdie."

I dropped the spell book to the ground, my hands shaking. "What kind of important news?"

"First and foremost, I'd like to introduce myself," she said airily, floating over to a headstone not far from Hazel's. "I'm Henrietta Hampton."

The way she was gesturing to the stone, I figured it must

be hers. But I couldn't quite make out what it said from this angle, and I stayed put.

"It's nice to er, meet you, Henrietta. Now... about that important news?"

She breezed back over to where I was, the bottom hem of her dress disappearing into the night as she did. "I'm limited in my movement. If I'd been able to, I would've warned you much sooner, child," Henrietta said, still edging around the circle in a sort of ethereal float. "But you rarely come out here far enough for me to have the chance. It's why I've been using as much of my energy as I can, to pulse my existence further away from the cemetery here, and into your home. I thought perhaps if I did it that way, you might just come outside to see what the fuss was about."

Well, that explained the chills I kept getting anytime I was in the kitchen... "I'm sorry I didn't realize sooner, Ms. Hampton. I've been a little preoccupied."

"Mm. I've noticed. There's been a lot of noise coming from inside the place. Not to mention what happened here."

I raised a brow. Something churned inside of me as I took a step forward, leaving the spell book on the ground. "You know about that?"

She nodded slowly. "Of course."

That's when it dawned on me. I brought my hand up to my mouth. "You were here. You saw?"

Henrietta turned away, the side-profile of her face glowing in the bit of moonlight that was poking through the clouds overhead. When she turned back to me, her eyes were dark holes. The light had gone out of them, though the rest of her was glowing even stronger than before.

What had I gotten myself into? I scrambled for the salt, keeping the big container of it in my hands as if it were a weapon.

"I saw. The scene is still fresh in my mind. He is *not*

welcome here. I shall not be as willing to do nothing as I was that night, if he steps one foot on the property."

My jaw dropped. "So it was a *he*… wait, if you were there and saw it all, why didn't you do anything? Are you even able to?"

Henrietta nodded again, but this time her eyes had returned to the silvery glow they were before. "I am. But I didn't because it's much harder these days, and I didn't want to use up all of my energy summoning to do the little bit that I can. Not when I knew I'd need it to communicate with you if things went south. Which they did."

Everything in me tensed. I had to remind myself that there wasn't much a spirit could really do to interfere with the living. "Who did it, then? It was a man, right?"

"It was. And he has been around here more than once. I thought something might have been off with him, but I was genuinely surprised to see him driving up along the access road there that night." Her ghostly fingers were pointing to the side road that nearly split my property from Willa-Mae's, with the exception of some live oaks that were dotted here and there between.

"Who? Who was driving up the road, Henrietta?"

She was clearly wrapped up in telling her own version of the events, completely ignoring what I was saying. "The car was swerving from the other end of the road as far as I could see. The headlights weren't on." Henrietta floated along to the next gravestone, her face solemn. "She was out there, though I couldn't see why. He didn't see her, and she couldn't see him until his car was upon her too fast. I couldn't tell, but at first it looked like he hit her with the side mirror on his car."

I saw it in my head, trying to puzzle it out. She'd been hit by a car? But Sheriff Paine didn't mention anything about there being any evidence of that…

"Go on," I said.

"But then again she hadn't fallen, so I figured he must have just startled her. The car stopped several paces ahead, right there where the street ends. He got out of it, slamming the door shut. There was such an unpleasantness to him... and it surprised me."

I frowned. "Why did it surprise you? Have you seen the man before?"

"She was already walking over, mad as a hissing cat, and fussing at him. It was the middle of the night and he was yelling for her to be quiet before she woke the whole neighborhood."

"That can't be right. I'm sorry. You must have it wrong— the Sheriff told me the time of death given on Willa-Mae's medical examination came back that she was killed around 7:00 PM or so, not the middle of the night." And here I thought she was actually going to give me some accurate information...

I could see the expression in Henrietta's face change. She didn't like being told she was wrong.

"It was as I've told you. I was there, you were not. Now, Willa-Mae and this man were really getting into it, arguing over something more than him nearly hitting her with his car. There was something about her house mentioned, though I wasn't close to hear it very well."

I sighed. "Okay. And then what?" I really didn't want to spend all night waiting for the answer to the most important question of all.

"He pulled her against him, somehow tripping her feet out from under her. He caught her, spun her around, and did something with his arm— they were facing away from me though I saw her struggling to get out of his grip. He was strangling her with his arm, I think." The last couple of sentences came out of Henrietta's mouth in a frenzied whisper. What she'd seen was just as shocking to her as it was to me.

It was hard not to imagine the scene playing out that way, but it paired with what Sheriff Paine had said. "Did you see him, though, Henrietta?"

She floated up until the only thing that really separated us was the circle. I could make out more of her features. She had the weathered face of someone who'd been around nearly as long as I have.

I wonder when she was born...

"The man. He's not allowed here anymore. I get such a bad feeling from him, Birdie. He's full of lies."

The man? I fought my way through the words. "Wh-which one?"

She stared at me for a moment. "The one who is your friend. Who brought you to this place to begin with."

It clicked a moment or two later.

Oh, no.

Oh, no.

I wasted no time worrying about the possibilities of opening the salt circle— I bent down and swiped the salt out of the way to make enough room for me. Leaving everything behind, I rushed around the corner of the house, nearly running into the gazebo.

The streetlights were on in the cul de sac, and I could see the asphalt sparkling under the lights. It was quiet, save for my feet pounding the pavement. I was out of breath within a minute of running, not having to sprint like that in so many years.

It took me a moment to realize where I was headed, and a minute later I was standing outside the red door, banging on it.

From somewhere inside the house, a voice called out, "Just a minute!"

I nearly bowled Ruby over as she opened the door with a bright smile. "Oh, Birdie! It's so nice to—oh my!"

I hated being rude, but this was simply no time for manners. "Where's your mama, dear? I need to speak with her, right away."

"Is everything all right?"

Geena walked around the corner from where I knew her kitchen to be. "What's got you all in a bother, Birdie?"

My chest was seizing against the breath I was trying to take again, and I took a moment to catch it before locking eyes with her. "I figured it out. I know… I know what happened."

She exchanged a look with Ruby. "What on earth are you talking about?"

"Sorry, Birdie," Ruby said, peeking her head around me. "We have company, actually. Mama, could you maybe chat with her in your bedroom?"

I smacked my hand to my forehead. Of course they did—it wouldn't be me unless something got in the way.

"Sorry Ruby, I didn't mean to barge in and interrupt you and your…" but my voice trailed off.

Sitting on their couch, briefcase and paperwork spread out on the coffee table in front of him, was none other than the person I'd come to warn them about.

Gregory Barnaby.

Every ounce of blood in my body ran cold.

He regarded me with the same polite smile he always had, ever since the day I walked into his office to buy my house. "Birdie! Lovely to see you. I trust everything's okay over there?"

It was like trying to find a needle in a haystack, looking for the proper words to reply with. I had to pretend as if everything was okay and that I wasn't suddenly aware of the fact that Gregory was Willa-Mae's murderer.

Ruby and Geena were both looking at me funny until I

finally managed to speak up. "Sorry," I said, clearing out the thick feeling in my throat. "It's nice to see you as well, dear. Like I said, I didn't mean to intrude on whatever's going on here."

"Gregory's just helping me with this silly idea I've got in my head," Ruby laughed, breaking the odd tension I'd created.

"Not at all silly, you mean," he corrected her, pointing down to the paperwork. "We've got some real potential here. I'm glad you called me over to come take a look."

"I'm thinking of renting an office," she went on to explain. "I haven't quite figured out for what yet, I mean there are so many ideas floating around in my mind that it's hard to make heads or tails of them, but..." she said, still smiling at me. "I found a few places and wanted an expert opinion."

"And Gregory, being the expert of course," I said, doing my best not to sound as forced as it all felt. I was still stuck in fight or flight mode, and what was worse was that two of my friends had no idea.

I had to figure out a way to tell Geena, at least.

Speaking of Geena... she was still staring at me funny. "Are you sure everything's okay?" she asked softly.

Ruby took a seat next to Gregory, and my heart raced. It would be only so easy for him to reach over and strangle her, too.

I nodded but knew I couldn't say the word. And she didn't seem to be buying it, anyway.

I needed to tell her somehow, and fast.

I waited until Gregory fully had his back to me before I pointed at him, my eyes wide. "It's him!" I tried to mouth, doing my best.

Geena frowned, squinting. She had the common sense enough to not call attention to me though, and I grit my teeth.

Oh. Of course!

Concentrating my absolute hardest, I envisioned exactly what I wanted Geena to see. I didn't want to startle Ruby, who was now offering Gregory some cookies anyway, so I stuck to strictly Geena.

In my mind, I fogged up the large front windows that had the drapes already drawn open. I imagined an invisible hand tracing large words on the foggy glass panes.

"He Killed Her."

Geena gasped, and all eyes were on her. She blinked, obviously realizing her mistake, and tried to laugh it off anyway. "Sorry. I thought I saw a big black spider on the window. Carry on."

I couldn't see Gregory's expression from my angle, but I could tell he was tensing up. Sort of as if he knew to be wary of us.

She jutted her chin toward where her two bedrooms were. "Come on, Birdie. We can chit-chat in my room while they talk business." She said it with a wink at Ruby, but even I could see how it lacked her usual warmth.

The two of us scuttled into the bedroom where I promptly shut the door.

Geena stood barely a few feet away, pulling her cardigan tighter around herself. She looked absolutely spooked.

"It's a long story to explain," I began, keeping it low, "but I know it was him. There was a… a witness."

"No!"

I nodded. "Yes, ma'am. And they saw the whole thing. Apparently he was driving down the access road there and nearly hit Willa-Mae with his car. The two of them got into it I think, and he ended up putting her into some kind of chokehold and suffocated her. Honest to God, Geena, that's what happened." I held up my crossed fingers.

She let out a long breath and started to pace the freshly cleaned carpet. "I just… I can't fathom it. Him? *Gregory*? We all know him, though!"

"I know it."

"And he… he's the good one!"

I shrugged. "Apparently the apples didn't really fall far from one another after all."

She shook her head in disbelief, stopping to sit down on the edge of her bed. "I just can't believe it… How in the world did we not know?"

Truth be told, I hadn't given it much thought in the past ten minutes since I'd found out. "I don't know. I only just found out about it myself."

There was a soft knock at the door.

"Just a second, honey," Geena called out before dropping her chin into her hands.

Ruby knocked again, this time a little louder.

Geena looked back up. "Oh for Pete's sake, girl. Birdie, do you mind?"

I nodded and pulled the door open, sighing.

Ruby wasn't alone.

In fact, Gregory was the one who must have knocked, because he had her pinned in some sort of strange hold in front of him, her eyes wide and her arms away from her body. The scarf she'd been wearing was half stuffed into her mouth.

I sucked in a breath.

The light had gone from his eyes, replacing it with something more sinister.

He smiled a wicked smile. "I think we all need to have a little talk in the living room."

20
BINGO

"Ruby! Get your hands off of her!" Geena screeched like some kind of wild animal and rushed at him from the bed.

She stopped dead in her tracks when Gregory tightened his grip around her neck. Ruby's eyes were filled with tears and they widened even more.

I grabbed at Geena around her waist to pull her backward, my brain kicking into overdrive.

Gregory nodded his head back toward the living room. "Go on. Sit down before you regret it."

The strong fumes of alcohol rolled off his breath, eerily reminding me of the supposed rum cake...

We carefully shuffled into the living room, holding on to each other for dear life. I was so worried she'd try to make a dive for Gregory that I still kept my arms around her. It wouldn't do a darn bit of difference if Ruby's neck was broken in the process.

Both of us sat shaking like leaves as Gregory yanked Ruby back over to where we were. "So you finally put it together, did you? And here I had you pegged for some kind of loon."

I knew he was only trying to get a rise out of me, but he

was doing a pretty good job, all things considered. The sneer on his face alone was enough to make me want to kick him right where it hurts.

"Why are you doing this?" I asked, looking between him and Ruby. "Let her go—she has nothing to do with this."

He simply rolled his eyes. "I know how hostage situations work, Birdie. So no, I don't think I will."

I seethed, but Geena's leg shook against mine and I bit my tongue. I didn't want to make the situation worse with my smart mouth.

"It's a shame I have all these loose ends to tie up now," he sighed, yanking Ruby back some more until they were against the corner of the room. "I'm not really all that creative… but it looks like I'll have to get creative to get rid of three different bodies."

Ruby shook and cried out against the scarf in her mouth, writhing to get away. Geena whimpered, but the look on her face was one of pure determination.

I needed to get us out of this and fast. So I did what I did best.

"Why did you do it?" I whispered. "Why did you kill Willa-Mae?"

Gregory barked a laugh. "I'm surprised anyone really needs a solid answer there. I mean, this is Willa-Mae Hurst we're talking about. The nastiest old biddy in Nella. The question should be why didn't I do it *sooner*?"

I shook my head, playing into the shocked, feeble-minded thing he thought I was. "Oh, that's a terrible thing to say. No one deserves to go like that."

And just like that, I cracked him open.

"You don't think so? You just moved here, and you think you already know everything about everything, do you? Why, I'll have you know that your no-good neighbor was far more interested in what all you were doing than you might realize. That morning I even overheard her telling some other lady in the super-market about you being a lesbian with a secret lover in the neighborhood. She was speculatin' mighty hard."

That little scheming woman... "She'd never," I said.

"If you say so."

I pretended to clear my throat. "And even if she did, what's so bad about that anyway? It's 2019, after all. Is it true? No. Did she deserve to die for possibly telling people something like that? Also, no."

He shook his head. "That's the thing though. She did deserve it. I didn't think so at first, in fact I was feeling pretty guilty about the whole thing. But the more I think about it, the better I feel. Nella is better without that miserable woman."

I glanced sideways at Geena, wishing I could somehow make her feel better. "And why is that?"

"She screws people over, that's why!" he rasped. "She screwed me over, she's screwed my brother over—and she's willing to do it with a damn smile on her face!" He didn't even look like himself anymore, but rather like the deranged image I had in my head of his brother committing the murder.

"The bingo game," Geena said.

"What's that?" he growled.

"It's because of the bingo game, isn't it? You were mad because she won the house in the bingo game. I remember hearing about how you were rantin' and raving about it to anyone who'd listen."

Suddenly I remembered Gregory and Gus arguing in Cinda's bakery. Gus had mentioned something about Gregory *losing it all* in a bingo game, and Gregory had gotten snippy with him over it. And they'd even mentioned something about their wrestling meets... so that fit as well.

Was this what he was talking about?

"She had it rigged—I just know it. Someone felt bad for

her, living in that dump she was in. They took away my chance at flipping that place for some serious cashflow. I already had a third-party involved, in fact. I owed him when they dropped the house from auction… Now I owe him *thousands*. Though I'm sure it won't be a problem when both her house *and* the Hampton House go back on the auction block. What a nice little investment that would be!"

His grip loosened up on Ruby a little bit. I could see the bruising there already, and new flames licked at my insides, wanting to protect her and to take him down.

"There's one thing I don't understand though…" I began, keeping the formulating plan in the back of my mind still going. "The medical report said she was killed somewhere in the middle of the night. Yet you did this before then, didn't you?"

His eyes, which I only just realized were bloodshot, narrowed. "I did, not that it matters."

"So the medical report was wrong. She wasn't killed then, she was killed either right before or right after you stopped by my place. No wonder the cake smelled so strongly… it wasn't the cake. It was you. You were drinking and driving and nearly ran Willa-Mae over. And when she called you out on it, you decided the only logical thing to do was to kill her. Am I missing anything?" I said, ticking everything off on my fingers. I was nearly done, conjuring it up in my head…

Surprisingly, the idiot fell for it.

"The medical report wasn't wrong. Not really. Let's just say I have my ways…"

"And by ways, you mean your brother who just so happens to have access to the hospital's records?" Geena snapped.

The sneer on Gregory's face darkened to something else.

Quick to intervene, I wriggled my fingers out in front of me ever so carefully so as not to earn his attention. As badly as I wanted to close my eyes, I knew I couldn't. I wouldn't.

So that meant I had to pull together the best kind of screen I could, with my eyes wide open. And believe me, that's no easy feat.

Slowly inhaling through my nose, I picked a spot on the wall to stare at, letting the tunnel vision take over as fast as possible. I was aware of Gregory talking, but I couldn't make out what he was saying. It was like being underwater where everything was slow and muffled.

A long black snake wrapped around Ruby's leg, twisting its way up, though she was completely unaware. A second snake wasn't far behind, and it was at that moment that Gregory saw them.

"What the hell…?" I could hear him trying to shake them off of the both of them.

The room was hazy around me and all I could see was the screen I was inventing. I breathed deeply, trying not to seem out of place.

The third snake emerged from behind him out of nowhere, slithering around his own neck. It wasn't actually happening, of course. But that didn't make it any less real to Gregory.

He jerked away, shoving Ruby away from him, trying to grasp for the snake that wasn't really there. Screeching, he rammed shoulder-first into the curio and sent dozens of little figurines flying off their shelves, some of them breaking into tiny pieces.

Geena shrieked as she lunged forward, not to her daughter, but to the wrought-iron fire poker lying against the old brick fireplace. She swung at Gregory with a good thwack, and he fell forward, still yelling.

She knocked my concentration in the process, and Gregory, utterly confused, scrambled to his feet and pushed past her as she went for another hit.

"Mama!" Ruby screamed, running after Geena and yanking her back as hard as she could.

"I got him, Geena," I said as calmly as I could.

Ruby was still struggling to keep her mother back, but I was already on my feet at the door, watching Gregory try and regain his composure at the bottom of the three steps out the front door.

It was a long shot, and I couldn't even remember the last time I'd physically manifested my defense magic—or if I even could.

But concentrating hard, I twisted my fingers together, interlocking them before pushing the blue energy flowing through them outwards, arcing it to hit Gregory square in the back. Already dazed, he staggered forward right into the mailbox. With a loud thud, his head smacked the metal mailbox and Gregory fell to his knees before falling over to the side and into the little petunias Geena had growing around the bottom of the mailbox post.

I let out a breath I didn't even know I was holding in. With a sob, Ruby threw herself against me, her arms tightly around me.

"Oh my God," her voice scratched. "Thank you. Thank you."

I squeezed her gently, not wanting to potentially make her injury worse. "Shh, it's all right now, darling. Your mama and I will get it all straightened out. He'll never touch another hair on your pretty head, okay?"

I felt her nod against me, but she wasn't letting go anytime soon.

Geena's voice drifted above the scene a moment later. "Yes, I need Sheriff Paine on the phone right this minute. Well I'm sorry, Timothy, but it's incredibly urgent and if you don't put him on this phone, so help me I will tell everyone in church how Pastor Thomas caught you and his daughter baptizing each other just a few weeks back. That's right. Mmhmm. Thank you, kindly." She narrowed her eyes at me and gave me a nod. "We'll get this piece of trash off my lawn faster than a hot knife through butter, believe you me."

"A*re you ready?*" someone cheered from over by the grill.

Everyone turned their heads and row after row of people started pumping their fists in the air. Whistles let out into the late October sky, and the bonfire's flames seemed to climb higher.

"Hotty toddy, gosh almighty! Who are we? Hey! Flim-flam, bim-bam. Ole Miss, yes ma'am!" more than half the tailgaters shouted back.

I giggled as Max and Eva joined in with their little arms and fists waving back and forth like the rest of them.

"Looks like the first tailgate of the season is off to a grand ol' start, huh?" Geena bumped my hip with hers and winked, carrying the next pot of chili out to the four tables we'd all pushed together for the pre-game party.

I grinned. "All right. It isn't so bad." Football wasn't really my thing, but around here College Football was on a whole 'nother level. And I wasn't about to miss out on a party like this one.

Everyone was walking around in powder blue and red baseball caps, some people even wearing those goofy foam fingers with the words, 'Ole Miss' on them. It was a sight to behold, truly. Never had I seen so many people gathered like this, spread out across three different yards.

It was Cinda's idea, initially. Her and her husband John had set up the big projector outside in their beautiful back-yard, ready to do some grilling and watch the University of Mississippi apparently 'whoop some tail,' as John had put it.

The smell of hotdogs grilling started drawing everyone

out, and before long, the whole neighborhood was outside, tailgating together.

In the corner, Frannie, Cinda, TJ, Geena, and me were rehashing the craziest story to come out of Nella yet.

"I'm just happy they took him in," Frannie said, shuddering. "It scares the bejeezus out of me to think that he was right under our very noses this whole time."

"At least he got what he deserves," Cinda said, folding her arms across her chest. "His tail ain't going nowhere now."

"Both of them, you mean," TJ amended. "Let's not forget that by the grace of the man upstairs, Gregory's rotten brother got thrown in the slammer, too."

"Very true," I said, doing my best not to smile. I'd been so furious at myself for condemning a so-called innocent man as a murderer thanks to my instinct, that now I felt a little vindicated. I knew something was off about Gus...

A cute commercial came booming along on the big projector in Cinda's backyard, startling me even over all the noise. *Why in the world do they do that with commercials?* I may have been one hundred and thirty-three, but I certainly wasn't *deaf*.

"Oh my goodness, look at him!" Cinda squealed in a baby voice. A huge fluffy dog was prancing around in some kind of dog kibble commercial. "I love big dogs!"

"He reminds me a little of Duke, wasn't it? Hazel's old Great Dane?" Frannie asked.

Wait.

My head whipped around. "Did you say a Great Dane? As in the dog?"

Frannie looked at me funny. "Well yes. Hazel had a Great Dane. He was a great big ol' thing, too. Likely to knock you on your rear if he got too excited. Why?"

I glanced back toward my house. "What did he look like?"

"He was a pretty gray color mainly, but he had white

around his paws." Geena smiled softly. "Hazel always said his paws looked like little socks."

"He was like a gentle giant, I thought. Hazel missed him so, so much. She got him when she first got married, in fact. I can't even remember how many years it's been since he died," Cinda added.

"Well I'll be darned. Huh," I said, putting it all together slowly.

Geena, Frannie, Cinda, and TJ all frowned at once, but I played it off as coyly as possible. "I used to have a Great Dane. I called him… Grifter. He was a wily thing, too."

The conversation kept going, with TJ and Cinda doing their usual arguing over something dumb, but I was left with more questions.

My Grifter… not even alive? Part of me was certainly sad about it, it really did feel like it came out of left field.

But a bigger part of me, and the part where my witchy instincts tended to kick in, knew something had been sort of odd about the whole thing. No one else ever seemed to notice him, and as big of a thing as he was, I never saw him eat.

In that moment, all I wanted to do was love on him. Bless his soul, I hadn't even known this whole time…

But to give me the benefit of the doubt, never in my life had I heard of an actual animal ghost. We'd always been taught that only humans had the ability to become spirits… and it only made me wonder just how little we really knew as magical beings.

With more and more people coming out of the broom closet each day, I figured we were due for some kind of better formal training—though I had very little time or space in my own brain to give it much thought. I'd been lucky to get out of Grandmother's house with a lick of sense to me.

I saw Ruby sipping from her beer bottle, leaning up against the trellis covered in ivy.

"Hey you," I said strolling over and figuring now was the best time to talk.

Even though a week had already gone by since Sheriff Paine and the whole darn sheriff's department swarmed Witch Hazel Lane, I hadn't had much of a chance to talk to Ruby. And considering that she was a smart girl and had figured out the truth about me being a witch after seeing me in action, I knew it was a conversation we needed to have.

It only took me a few words in before she immediately had cut me off.

"Not another word about any of that, now. Your secret is as safe with me as it is with Mama. I won't say a thing to anyone, I promise."

I raised a brow, surprised at how easy this was turning out to be. "Not even Shawn?"

She shook her head. "Not even to him. It's not my secret to tell, and I'll do well to remember it. Besides, Birdie. You saved our lives. I'll probably spend the rest of my life thanking you for it. Not to mention, I mean… I just have so many questions! How do your powers work, for starters?" she dropped her voice to barely above a whisper and leaned in to ask.

All I could do was chuckle. "My dear, there will be plenty of time for all that. And like I said, your mama did a great lot of help getting that lowlife out of the house, too. You don't need to thank me any more than you need to thank her. I've got your back, darlin'."

Max ran up and tugged at Ruby's shawl. "Mama. Can I have another bag of chips? Please?"

She ruffled his hair. "Ask your daddy. I'm talking to Ms. Devaine."

But I just waved her off. "It's okay, Ruby. I think right now I just want to spend some time with your mama and them, if that's okay."

Ruby beamed at me and gave me one last hug before letting Max take her hand and lead her away.

The whole neighborhood seemed brighter somehow. I looked around and smiled, before glancing back at my own house, set further back from the road than everyone else's. I imagined Grifter snoozing away, though now I wasn't so sure if he was ever really even asleep. Did ghost dogs sleep?

Geena threw her arm around me and nodded toward the house. "Not planning on leaving the party already, are you?"

"Me?" I said innocently. "I'd never. Besides, I think I'd rather just hang out here with my best friend. I hear she has some special chili recipe, but she won't share."

Geena pinched at me but laughed. "Keep it up and your best friend won't even let you lick the spoon."

Somewhere in Cinda's yard, someone scored a touchdown on our side. The whole neighborhood echoed with cheers and whistles for the rest of the day and well into the night.

The End.

Join Jerri's newsletter and receive three free books, three short stories, and more!

J. L.'s Mailing List
Facebook Page

Author's Note: I truly hope you enjoyed my book as much as I enjoyed writing it! If you enjoyed it, I'd be incredibly grateful if you could leave a short, honest review on Amazon. It can be as simple as a couple of sentences about why you liked the book. Reviews are crucial for any indie author – everyone of us depend on them!

ALSO BY J. L. COLLINS

Spell Maven Mystery Series Order:

Spell Maven from Spell Haven (Book 1)

Snitch Witch (Book 2)

Tragic Magick (Book 3)

Witch Hazel Lane Mystery Series Order:

Grits in the Graveyard (Book 1)

Devil on My Doorstep (Book 2)

Monsters Under the Magnolia (Book 3)

BUBBA-RAY'S CAROLINA PEACH SANGRIA

Carolina Peach Sangria

- One 750 ml. bottle Rosé Wine
- 3/4 cup peach or raspberry vodka
- 1 cup thawed frozen lemonade concentrate
- 3 large ripe peaches, peeled and chopped
- 1 1/2 cups fresh raspberries
- 2 cups chilled club soda
- ice, for serving

1. In a large pitcher, combine the wine, vodka and lemonade; stir. Add the peaches and raspberries. Cover and chill at least 6 hours, or until nice and cold (overnight is fine too).

2. Just before serving, stir in the club soda

- If you'd rather use regular vodka, add 1/2 cup of peach or raspberry nectar to the recipe. You can find nectar in your market's juice aisle (look for KERNS nectar).
- Add a tablespoon or two of sugar if you'd like a sweeter sangria.

- This recipe can be easily doubled.
- If you are making this recipe as GLUTEN-FREE, just be sure to use a brand of lemonade concentrate that is known to be GF.

(Recipe from recipegirl.com)

GEENA'S HOMEMADE GREEN BEAN CASSEROLE

Green Bean Casserole

- 1 lb. Fresh Green Beans (ends snapped off)
  - 8 Tablespoons Salted Butter (divided)
  - 1 Large Onion (chopped)
  - 8 ounces Sliced Mushrooms
  - 3 cloves Garlic (minced)
  - 2 1/2 cups Half n Half
  - 1 teaspoon Salt
  - 1 teaspoon Pepper
  - 2 Tablespoons Flour or Cornstarch
  - 2 cups Fried Onions (such as French's)
  - 1/2 cup Parmesan Cheese, grated (optional)

1. In a large skillet, heat 4 Tablespoons of butter over medium-high heat. Add onions and cook until tender and caramelized, about 7-8 minutes, stirring often. Add mushrooms and cook for 4 minutes longer. Stir in garlic and cook for 1 minute. Transfer the mixture to a bowl.

2. After the onion-mushroom mixture has been removed,

use the same skillet. Heat skillet to a medium heat and add remaining 4 Tablespoons of butter. Add flour or cornstarch and begin to quickly whisk the mixture. Let cook, whisking often, for about 2 minutes. Stir in half-n-half, salt, and pepper. Cook for 4-5 minutes until mixture thickens. Taste and check for seasonings.

3. Preheat oven to 350 degrees. Bring a large pot of water to a boil. Add green beans and cook for 6-7 minutes. Drain and transfer to ice bath to cool (optional).

4. Add onion-mushroom mixture to cream sauce and stir. Add green beans and stir to coat. Sprinkle with parmesan cheese, if using. Pour into a 9 x 9 baking dish. Bake for 25 minutes or until bubbly. Remove from the oven and cover with fried onions. Bake for 5 minutes longer. Serve immediately, if possible.

• May use fresh, frozen or canned green beans. If using canned green beans, they don't need to be cooked ahead of time.

• Don't use anything less than half-n-half in these green beans as it creates a thick sauce.

• If you want bite-size green beans, cut the fresh green beans in half.

(Recipe from modernhoney.com)

RUM CAKE

Moist Rum Cake

For the Cake:

- 1/3 cup chopped walnuts or pecans
- 1 3/4 cups all-purpose flour
- 1/4 cup cornstarch
- 4 teaspoons baking powder
- 1 teaspoon kosher salt
- 4 large eggs, room temperature
- 3/4 cup whole milk, room temperature
- 3/4 cup dark rum
- 1 tablespoon vanilla extract
- 1/2 cup unsalted butter, at room temperature
- 1 1/2 cups granulated sugar
- 1/2 cup plus 3 tablespoons canola oil, divided
- 1 (3.4-ounce) package of instant vanilla pudding

For the Rum Syrup:

- 3/4 cup unsalted butter
- 1 1/2 cups granulated sugar
- 1/2 cup water

- 1 tablespoon light corn syrup
- Pinch of salt
- 1/2 cup dark rum

1. Adjust oven rack to lower-middle position and heat oven to 325 degrees. Grease and flour 12-cup nonstick Bundt pan. Sprinkle the chopped walnuts around the bottom; set aside.

2. Combine flour, cornstarch, baking powder, and salt in medium bowl.

3. In small bowl, whisk the eggs, milk, rum, 1/2 cup canola oil, and vanilla extract.

4. Using stand mixer fitted with paddle attachment, beat butter and sugar on medium-high speed until pale and fluffy, about 3 minutes. Add the flour mixture and the remaining 3 tablespoons of canola oil, and mix on medium-low speed until the mixture looks like wet sand, about 1 minute. Add the pudding mix and mix again on medium-low speed until combined. Add the egg mixture to the dry ingredients and beat on medium speed until thoroughly combined, about 2 to 3 minutes, scraping down the sides of the bowl as needed.

5. Pour the cake batter into the prepared Bundt pan and bake for 50 to 60 minutes, or until a toothpick inserted into the center of the cake comes out clean.

6. When the cake has about 10 minutes left to bake, start making the rum syrup. In a medium-sized saucepan over medium heat, melt the butter. Once it is melted, add the sugar, water, corn syrup and salt. Bring to a boil then reduce to a low simmer and cook for 5 minutes, stirring occasionally. Turn off the heat and stir in the rum. Once it is mixed in, return it to medium heat for about 30 seconds.

7. When the cake comes out of the oven, immediately pour one-third of the rum syrup over the bottom of the cake. Pour slowly so it has time to seep into the cake. Using a fork or a skewer, poke holes all over the bottom of the cake. Let it sit for 5 minutes.

8. Invert the cake onto a serving platter. Using a fork or a skewer, poke holes all over the cake (the top, sides, and around the inside). The holes ensure that the rum syrup seeps into the cake evenly. Very slowly pour the remaining rum syrup over the top of the cake, allowing it to drip down the sides. You want to do this step very slowly so that the syrup seeps into the cake and doesn't just pool on the bottom of the serving dish.

9. Allow the cake to cool to room temperature before serving. Leftovers can be kept, tightly wrapped, at room temperature for up to 5 days.

(Recipe from sweetpeaskitchen.com)

ABOUT THE AUTHOR

J. L. (Jerri) lives in the Lowcountry of South Carolina, with her family and feisty furbaby. She loves southern food, literally any dog, hiking, Carolina sunrises on the beach, shopping on King Street, and curling up with about twenty different books on the weekends. Her favorites are mysteries and fantasies where the characters make her laugh, cry, and feel #allthefeels. When she gets the rare chance, she also likes to go exploring and learning more about Charleston's rich history.

Made in the USA
Middletown, DE
10 September 2020